J URNEY TO NO END

A professional revolutionary is sent to help a group of working men holding an important factory from going into the hands of Eas Germany. He soon realises that even thou he has no political interest in the revolt, a series of incidents involve him deeply in the need for the factory to be returned back into Western hands. Having lost s faith during the Spanish Civil War he ds it again in the revolt of these wo g men: this time his faith is not in po s but in people...

JOURNEY TO NO END

JOURNEY TO NO END

by

Charles Whiting

Dales Large Print Books
Long Preston, North Yorkshire,
BD23 4ND, England.

British Library Cataloguing in Publication Data.

Whiting, Charles
    Journey to no end.

    A catalogue record of this book is
    available from the British Library

    ISBN   978-1-84262-793-8 pbk

First published in Great Britain in 1957 by Jonathan Cape

Copyright © 1957 Charles Whiting

Cover illustration © Mohamad Itani by arrangement with
Arcangel Images

The moral right of the author has been asserted

Published in Large Print 2010 by arrangement with
Mrs Gillian Tidmus-Whiting

Dales Large Print is an imprint of Library Magna Books Ltd.

Printed and bound in Great Britain by
T.J. (International) Ltd., Cornwall, PL28 8RW

PROLOGUE WITH DEATH

CHAPTER ONE

From the factory on the hill came the shrill of the siren.

Everywhere the men were climbing out of the thick brown water of the lock. Von Korn-feld laid his shovel on the muddy grass verge and heaved himself up and out of the grey mud that sucked at his battered boots. The trucks were coming again. They could not see them yet, but they could hear them plainly, grinding their way up the steep gradient that led to the little town.

Schulze, the ganger, came out of his lean-to, pencil stuck behind his ear. The labourers in their battered, flabby boots moved past him towards the road.

'Hey, where do you tulips think you're off to?' he shouted.

Nobody answered him. He planted him-self in the way, but they pushed by him, their eyes fixed on the road along which the trucks would come. He tried to hold on to

9

one of the labourers, but the man raised his shovel and Schulze let go. He stopped old Krause.

'Ewald, where art thou going? Man, where art thou going?'

Hartmann pushed his way between them.

'Hey, what gives here?' Schulze bellowed, enraged.

'You can kiss me where I am beautiful and have no nose!' Hartmann shouted and went on. Krause followed him.

Schulze went back into his lean-to and took up the ancient telephone.

Overhead the sky was leaden and oppressive. The air was thick and made breathing an effort. All along the cobbled street the women, with their shopping-nets, had stopped and were gossiping, looking at the corner every now and again expectantly. The children, who had run out of the little school, followed by their teacher's protests, faltered, stopped and fell silent, oppressed suddenly by their elders' seriousness.

Hartmann, in the front rank of the waiting labourers, his eyes full of hatred, bent down and levered up one of the cobbles with his chisel. Other men began to follow his example.

The first truck came round the corner, its

engine grumbling at the hill, which never seemed to end, and the weight it was forced to carry. Along the street an angry murmur ran from group to group. The young men – thirty of them packed into the back of the truck like cattle for the market – stared out listlessly at the crowd and then dropped their eyes, as if ashamed. The fur-capped guard with the long bayonet looked straight ahead expressionlessly.

'More of 'em for the factory,' the words passed from mouth to mouth.

'Where you from, lads?' somebody shouted.

'From the East!' a dirty, light-haired boy shouted back.

'From the East!' the crowd repeated the words, as if they were of importance. 'From the East!'

The first truck rumbled past and a second one turned the corner, closely followed by a car full of officers with great square epaulets.

Suddenly a woman took a roll from her net and threw it into the second truck. A tall, wolfish-looking boy caught it neatly and began tearing at the tough, shiny skin with big white teeth. Other women opened their bags and began doing the same. The men

11

started to throw single cigarettes and cheap working-men's cigars.

An officer, with golden epaulets, leaned out of the car and bellowed at the young guard at the back of the truck. The soldier went red and levelled his long bayonet at the crowd, shouting something in his own tongue. The women moved back from the kerb. Someone somewhere began to boo. Everyone took it up. It grew louder and louder, so that it drowned the roar of the motors. Hartmann threw his cobble-stone. It hit the windscreen of the officers' car. The driver braked hard, skidded and crashed into a lamp-post. For a moment a great silence fell on the crowd as they realized what they had done, and then, as if they had broken invisible bands, they surged forward – men, women and children.

Eight or nine young men with long, untidy hair and shapeless pullovers seized the officers' car and began to shake it from side to side, lifting it higher and higher from the ground every time. The officer with the gold epaulets tried to draw his pistol. One of the young men reached in awkwardly and hit him squarely in the face so that the blood spurted from his nose and upper lip. A last heave and the car overturned with a splintering of glass and a crack of coachwork. Petrol began to escape from the engine. Someone set light to a sheet of newspaper and, shielded by many hands, the paper was passed forward to the youths. One of them threw it into the petrol and jumped back quickly. The petrol exploded into blue flames with a roar that sucked back the air. A great cheer went up from the crowd. This time there was no hesitation. They were committed. There would be no backing-out now.

Hartmann ran for his shovel. 'Kommt Jungs! The shovels!' he shouted as he ran towards the lock.

The trucks were braking sharply as they came round the corner. One driver didn't brake in time and went straight into the plate-glass window of the State Shop. Another rammed the back of its predecessor round the bend. Everywhere there was shouting and confusion.

The officers crawled from the burning car to the kicks and blows of the crowd. The one with the gold epaulets cleared a path for himself with his pistol, his hand, full of blood, held to his nose.

The fur-capped soldiers had begun jumping from the confusion of vehicles and were

13

forming a ragged line across the road.

'Quick, at the swine!' a woman screamed.

The crowd moved forward, the lock labourers grasping their shovels. Von Kornfeld found himself pushed forward between Hartmann and the old man, Krause. As they pressed forward, he was laughing softly inside. It was funny, he thought, to die like this. All his forefathers would have been leading the men holding the rifles at the other end of the street. And he was with the mob. He had no more time to think about the irony of the situation. One of the long-haired youths had run forward and slapped a fur-capped soldier across the face. He received the butt-end of a rifle in his stomach. He gave a half-shout, half-belch and went down on his knees, holding his stomach.

The crowd stumbled into a run. Stones flew through the air. The fur-capped soldiers looked at their officer. He was very white. He was only a young man. He hesitated. A cobble-stone hit one of the leading soldiers and sent him moaning to the ground. The officer nodded and ran quickly to the end of the line. And they fired. A weak, ragged volley, but it was enough. A man clasped his knee, saw the blood spurt through his clenched fingers and began to

14

cry. The crowd wavered, people at the front coming to a stop.

'Don't let the bastards scare yer!' Hartmann bellowed and waved his shovel.

And then suddenly the crowd broke and started to run, fighting and clawing at each other to get out of the soldiers' line of fire. Somebody gave Von Kornfeld a push in the small of the back, and he found himself running with the rest. He saw Krause stumble on the cobbles, and he caught the old man just before he fell. They ran on together. Gradually the crowd's pace slackened, and finally they stopped altogether when they reached the end of the main street where it narrowed and became an alley. Pressing themselves into doorways and against walls, they waited, their chests heaving with the exertion of running. The fur-capped soldiers knelt and waited too. From the direction of the People's Police barracks came the sound of sirens, growing louder and louder every moment.

'Die Vopos!' the crowd murmured.

The 'Ueberfallkommando' arrived. A squad of blue-uniformed People's Police, armed with short carbines, jumped from the high, armoured truck. The squad leader ran across to the officer with the gold epaulets and reported. Quickly the police spread out from one end of the street to the other, their carbines held across their bodies, tight to the chest. They began to advance slowly, while behind them the fur-capped soldiers relaxed, getting up and stamping their numbed feet on the ground.

The police moved down the deserted street, stepping carefully over the litter of shopping bags,shovels, packets that the crowd had dropped. The distance between them and the crowd grew less. Every step of their nailed boots rang out in the silence and echoed up between the tall, old-fashioned buildings. Somebody dropped a shovel with a clatter, and Von Kornfeld felt his heart jump high in his body like a startled girl. Krause took his arm and pressed it hard just above the muscle.

'It's our Dieter,' he whispered.

Von Kornfeld caught a glimpse of the tense white face of Dieter Krause, who had volunteered for the Barracked People's Police Six months before. And then the crowed were running again, vanishing into the side streets; the sound of their shoes, clattering over the cobbles, lingering in the chasm of a street long after they had gone...

The police relaxed against the wall and watched the trucks go by up the hill towards the factory. Here and there a man was smoking, although no order granting permission to do so had been given. Lieutenant Todt looked at their lazy attitudes with disgust, and squeezing his pince-nez a little more firmly on his nose, turned to his superior, Captain Wagner, who was watching the man with the shattered knee being bandaged. Captain Wagner's collar was undone and his hands were thrust deep into his trouser pockets.

Todt cleared his throat and clicked his heels together smartly. Police Manual. Theme: Behaviour in the Presence of Superior Officers, Wagner thought, but didn't turn.

At the second attempt Wagner turned round and looked at Todt, with his broad, good-humoured face. With a practiced flick of his thick worker's thumb and forefinger, he pushed his peaked cap to the back of his head.

'Na Todt. Wat is denn?' he asked.

'Request permission to clear the alleys, Comrade Captain?' Todt rapped out.

Wagner looked at Todt hard. He didn't like the lieutenant with his white gloves and his precise manner. He didn't like him with his

17

fervent look and his pale white face. He didn't like him with his pince-nez, which he had taken to wearing in imitation of the Great Man.

'Why, Comrade Lieutenant?'

'Teach 'em a lesson. Clear 'em and teach 'em a lesson. Some of them have been spoiling for this for a long time. We've had too many incidents in the last month.'

'You used all of eight words in the last sentence, Todt,' Wagner said and tried to make a joke of it, but Todt did not smile. His pale, rigid face showed no emotion.

Suddenly Wagner was angry with him.

'Look, man,' he said quietly, so that the men did not hear. 'You've still got egg-shell behind yer spoons! What do you expect them to do? They see their own folk dragged off to work in some factory run by a foreigner, and you expect them to give three cheers! Heaven, arse and cloud-burst, wake up, man!'

He controlled himself. 'They don't understand these things, Todt. It's your duty to help them to understand. Get out in the boozers and tell them. Don't talk to me about clearing the alleys!'

Todt went slightly paler than he was already. He adjusted his pince-nez again.

Little bourgeois swine, the captain thought. 'As you say, Comrade Captain,' he said slowly. And there was something about him at that moment which rather frightened Wagner. He shrugged it off and pulled his cap down. He looked hard at Todt. He detested these correct ones, who always had their hair the correct length, whose boots were always highly polished, who never needed a shave in the afternoon, who always knew the correct attitude of the moment.

'You can go, Comrade Lieutenant!' he said sharply.

'And the prisoner, Comrade Captain?' Todt asked.

'The prisoner?'

Todt nodded at the man with the shattered knee.

'Oh, him,' Wagner said. 'Krueger's lad. He's had a noseful. He can go home when they've patched him up.'

Wagner fancied for a moment that he saw hard lumps of muscles bunch and clench around Todt's jaw.

'Himmel, Arsch und Wolkenbruch!' he exploded, and then controlled himself quickly. 'Don't worry, man. Everything'll be all right now. Don't worry...'

2

But the captain was wrong. The little town on the hill seemed to contract like a man slinking into a side-street to avoid recognition. In the workers' pubs the Skat games and the newspapers, hanging along the walls by their hooks, were neglected. The usual noisy conversation had died overnight. Men sat in corners, talking in low tones, ceasing every time the felt curtains at the entrance were thrown back; they sat with their backs to the walls, feeling secure like that.

At home they shouted when someone entered at night and left the door open: 'Man, shut the door quick! Or have you got sacks standing outside?'

And everywhere they began their conversations with the warning: 'Sprich durch die Blume, mensch – speak through the flower man. Watch your talk!'

At nights the narrow cobbled streets of the town were silent except for the measured pacing of the police. One morning they found the body of a People's Policeman half-submerged in the green scum of the canal. There was no indication of how he had met his death, except that his pistol was missing from its holster. The night after that the police began to patrol in pairs, with an armoured car mounting a searchlight, slowly cruising the silent, tense streets from dusk to dawn. Even the women no longer gossiped in the streets, preferring to make their purchases and get home at once. The State Shop was empty except for some official's or party member's wife, although it was the only place where one could get sugar that month. The children, too, lounged against the walls of the school yard in the breaks or talked secretly in corners, puzzled at their inability to enter into this new adult world that had suddenly been created all around them. But the trucks still roared their way up to the factory on the hill. And their officers, with their broad, shining epaulets, still went by in the big black foreign cars. And when the siren blew at the factory, the labourers in the lock, the women in the street, the children in the school seemed not to notice, but secretly their muscles tensed with the knowledge that it would be soon. And then it was June, and every day the sky was obscured with big black thunderclouds...

THE JOURNEY

CHAPTER TWO

They sat all around him; the young lieutenants with the political science degrees from Harvard; the captain with the '45 and the leather OD armband; the fat major, who was taking notes of what the general was saying. And beneath the big wall-map, with its drawn-back curtains, sat the general.

He is like most of their generals – when they don't look like business-men – Richard thought. His uniform fits him well and he has the usual tough face, but there's something unsoldierly about him for all that, as if he's making a conscious effort to keep the hard facial line.

'Okay, Richard, let's go through it again,' the general said. He grinned briefly. 'Just for the hell of it.'

'I'm to be dropped on the night of the fourth-fifth. I contact reception committee – called Von Kornfeld. Tall, thin, well-spoken, wearing dyed officer's greatcoat. Krause – an old man with a three-quarter-length jacket – and Hartmann. Smallish in a leather coat. He'll approach me first. They'll know me when I order rum grog. Meeting place – centre of town, Jaegersbrunnen.'

'Check,' the general said and formed a circle with his thumb and forefinger. Like they do in the pictures, Richard thought. He waited politely and then continued:

'On the seventeenth we will blow the factory as planned.'

'Yes,' the general said quickly. 'Don't give a damn how you do it, Richard. Just get that factory blown. Perhaps it's better that I shouldn't know. Blow it and you can take off straight back here.' He swivelled round in his chair and pressed the point of his pencil on the map. 'We'll pick you up there. You've got the map reference?'

Richard nodded.

'Fine.'

The general cleared his throat. 'Any questions, Richard?'

'When do I get paid?'

The general took it as a joke. He laughed heartily. 'Yeah. But seriously, Richard, we want that factory blown. They tell me the big boys in Bonn don't sleep right at night, thinking about it.'

'And what about the characters over there and their – revolution?'

The general shrugged his shoulders. 'Tell them to come and collect their T.S. slips some time. They're Krauts, ain't they?'

The major stopped writing for a moment, and the general gave him a little nod of confirmation.

'But that's off the record, Richard.' The major started writing again. 'Any of you guys got any questions?' He turned to his officers.

They shook their heads.

'That's a bunch of Joes for you,' the general said, extending his hand towards the officers. 'No yes-men there, Richard. Don't even say yes.'

Richard smiled.

'Okay boys let's call it a day,' the general said.

The major closed his notebook and put his pencil away. The captain with the OD armband hitched the Colt round to his belly so that he could sit back in his chair. The curtain was drawn across the map. The young lieutenants with the political science degrees from Harvard began to practice their Russian again.

The general got to his feet and began to unbutton his jacket.

25

'Been Stateside, haven't you, Richard?' he asked.

'Yes, landed Rhein-Main last Sunday.'

The general laid his jacket over the back of a chair neatly.

'What's the dirt from the Pentagon, Richard?'

'Just dirt,' Richard Burdon answered.

The general laughed. 'Just dirt. That's good, Richard. Hey, Terry!' he called to the major. 'Did you hear that? I asked Richard here what the dirt was from the Pentagon, and he said: "just dirt". Funny, eh?'

The major laughed politely. 'Yeah, very funny, sir.'

The general unzipped his slacks, holding on to the back of a chair. He was wearing loose blue-and-white-striped shorts. His legs were very white and hairless.

'You a citizen yet, Richard?' he grunted, bending down and pulling the slacks over his shoes.

'Yes, General.'

'Call me Bill.'

The general climbed into a pair of light slacks and had some difficult in zipping them up. He flushed and shouted the old joke about getting it caught in a zipper that Richard had heard in officers' clubs all over the world. The major broke off his conversation with the police captain again and laughed politely until the general bent over his slacks once more.

There was a knock on the door. The police captain pushed his Colt to his thigh again to indicate that he was on duty. He went over to the door and opened it. His own sergeant, with the 'Air Police' armband, stood there. The captain stood back to let him in, but the general shouted: 'Get his card, Charley. His card, Charley, for Christ's sake!'

The captain's thick neck went red, and he asked the man for his identity card, although he and the general saw the sergeant eight hours a day, six days a week. Satisfied, he allowed the man in. He placed the sheaf of papers he was carrying on the desk in front of the general.

The general stood and glanced through the correspondence quickly, signing a letter here and there and occasionally tabbing on a blue slip from the containers on his desk, labelled: OKAY. I'LL GO ALONG WITH YOU, or LET'S TALK.

'That's a good deal you've made,' the general said, looking up at him. 'One deal you'll never lose on, Richard.'

'What's that, General?'

27

'Bill.'

'Bill?'

'Becoming a citizen, Richard. These days you hear a lot of crap talked, son; but the States looks after its own.' He signed the last letter and took off his spectacles. 'Nothing against Europe, Richard. But it's had its day.'

'Yes, it's had its day.' Richard echoed the general's words.

The general handed the correspondence back to the waiting sergeant, who left the room, followed by the captain as far as the door. The room relaxed again.

The general was ready. 'Goin' fishing,' he said. 'A couple of the Joes are pickin' me up. We've got us a couple of bottles stashed away. Some fishin', huh?'

Richard Burdon agreed.

'What are you going to do, Richard – stay at the Base?'

It wasn't a question: it was a statement. Richard knew that. He wouldn't be able to get off the Base now until they pushed him into that plane on the evening of the fourth – citizen or no citizen.

'I guess I'll stay on the Base, General.'

'Swell – and Bill.'

'Sorry – Bill.'

'You got plenty of Script, then?'

Richard Burdon nodded. 'Thank you, Bill. I don't feel much like Frankfurt, anyway.'

The general smiled his tight-mouthed general's smile for a second and patted him on the shoulder. 'Hang one on for me tonight, boy,' he said, his face relaxed again. 'It'll take your mind off it.'

'I'll do that – Bill,' Richard Burdon said.

The general left and he watched him go. What does he know about it? he asked himself. Hang one on! My eye!

Richard lingered around, but none of them took any notice of him. The fat major and the police captain were deep in a discussion of the merits of the Heidelberg Lions and the Frankfurt Yankees. The Harvard men were still practicing their Russian.

He went, saying goodbye, but nobody seemed to hear. So what? he told himself angrily. You're being paid for the deal, aren't you? Do you expect them to kiss your fanny for you? He walked out; a tall, thin man with slightly stooped shoulders. He was so tall that people rarely looked at his eyes, and when they did they usually looked away quickly.

Richard walked into the land of the P.X. The huge padded-wall bar of the Officers' Club was already crowded with young

29

lieutenants in blue having a drink before going to their quarters. Most of them were drinking at the bar, feet resting on the foot-rail, but here and there was a group on the floor, glasses in hand, playing crap.

He sat in a corner and ordered a beer from the German waiter. It was good beer. Export. It cost only six cents a bottle. He started to work out the cost in pence, but gave it up the next instant. Dollars and cents were his money now, weren't they?

He had only been sitting there five minutes when one of the paid hostesses spotted him. She came over, thinking he was lonely. She sat down without being asked.

'Phew!' she sighed. 'My aching back. I must walk kilometers in this place!'

Automatically he ordered her a drink and they sat there talking for a while. She spoke without a trace of accent. One might have supposed she came from the Coast.

'You new on the Base?' she asked. 'From Stateside?'

He nodded.

'What's the dirt from the Pentagon?'

'Just dirt.'

She laughed dutifully.

'You speak good English,' he said.

She frowned. She obviously did not like to

be reminded of the fact that she did not really belong. The fact amused Richard Burdon.

'Don't sweat, G.I.,' she came back with the soldiers' joke. 'I learn my English at school.'

He ordered another round.

'Where do you come from?' she asked.

They always wanted to know where you came from, he thought. Probably they wanted to measure you up with the archetype they saw in the cinema. For a moment he toyed with the idea of telling her he came from Texas and seeing what she made of that.

'Nowhere, I suppose. I only became a citizen last year. I'm mostly over here in Europe.'

'Oh.' She was surprised, but still interested. She would be wanting to hear how he made it into Paradise.

'I was English once,' he answered her unspoken question.

'Oh.'

She gave him another few minutes, but it was obvious that she had lost interest. They finished their drinks and he offered to buy a fresh round, but she refused.

'Mit mir ist kein Blumenpott zu gewinnen, was? You won't win a flower-pot with me,' he said with a smile.

31

'No.' She repeated the phrase in her own language, giving the words a slight American accent.

She got up and left. He watched her go over to a young air force captain sitting alone. She'd get to Paradise all right, he told himself. And by the way she's going it would be pretty soon.

The bar filled up. One or two of the older officers with their wives drifted in, their arms loaded with the tall, narrow packages from the P.X. For a time Richard chatted with a major, who had just been posted from France. He was still going through the rapturous stage that they all went through when they came to Germany – except the Jews, of course. He was glad to escape from the Frogland. They were worse than the dinges. Wild horses wouldn't drag him there again. Give it back to the parley-vous. Now, the Krauts...

Richard had a few more beers. He told himself he'd get nice and tired before he returned to his room.

In the next alcove a woman was telling another about a wife in 'Officers' Block D', who had bought a tin of Russian salmon on the 'economy' – they talked as if the local market belonged to another world. Nobody in the block was speaking to her, of course. Putting dollars out for them to buy guns to use against us like that! And have you seen the way she talks to the Negras? No feeling of class solidarity at all! The two women looked at each other indignantly. One of them glanced across at Richard for confirmation of their righteousness. Richard looked away and finished his beer. He paid and went.

The Base was pretty deserted. It was Saturday night, and everyone would be down in Frankfurt. He nodded to the white-capped policeman at the entrance to his block. All the same, the man asked for his identity card, although he had spent half an hour with him that morning translating for him to the boilerman. The policeman scrutinized the pass and then handed it back.

'Regulations, sir,' he said. 'Thanks for this morning.'

'Regulations – yeah.'

He undressed and got into the brown-blanketed iron bed. Somewhere a radio was playing out of an open window. It was quite far away. He switched out the light above his head. Somebody walking by the block gave a wolf-whistle. Probably at one of the hefty girls in their wooden slippers who worked in the G.I. Mess-hall. It was private and some-how sad, and it told him again that he was out of things.

After a time he fell asleep. He dreamt again. He dreamt that they had come for him in the middle of the night and when they had awakened him he had answered in the wrong language. The enormity of his mistake woke him again, as it always did.

He had been dreaming this dream for many years now. Always the same, except that with the years the uniforms had changed.

He went to sleep again and forced himself to dream the dream he always kept for the bad nights. They were coming down the dusty, glaring white road again. His shirt-back was soaked with sweat and the sling of his rifle cut into his shoulder and the tassel of the little foreign cap bumped up and down on his forehead irritatingly like some irksome fly. Down below he saw it again: the short, secret stretch of bright yellow sand at the base of the sheer white cliffs, and then the house with the black roof against the deep blue of the sea.

Here he always tried to make the dream last, but he never succeeded. There was always the sudden chatter of the machine-guns of the ambush and the scramble for the rocks, with Chalky White and the Russian left silent – sprawling in the thick white dust of the road. Richard Burdon turned over on his side and began to snore.

CHAPTER THREE

It was five o'clock. Von Kornfeld got out of bed at once and lit the rusty stove. He put on the cracked white coffee-pot with the remains of the night-before's coffee. Then he shaved and washed, scrubbing carefully under the armpits. Sitting on the bed, he pulled on his mud-stiffened trousers that could have stood up of their own accord. He inspected the soles of his boots, and decided he would need some more cardboard soon. He folded up a sheet of newspaper and pressed it into the left boot. Getting up, he went over to the wall to comb his hair. Stuck in the corner of the mirror was a cutting from an illustrated paper. It showed the passing-out parade of a Spandau Military Academy in 1934. With the aid of a magnifying glass borrowed from his landlady, he had discovered himself on the photograph. Every time he looked at it he automatically tried to brace his shoulders and then, just as automatically, remembered that since Crete he would never be able to brace his shoulders again. 'I shall move that damned photo tonight,' he promised himself, as he promised himself every morning.

It was five-twenty. He poured the coffee into a cup, using a piece of rag to sieve it, and ate the three slices of black bread that he had buttered the night before. He drank another cup of the coffee and smoked half a cigarette, containing the strong black Marhorka. They were the cheapest kind – the only ones he could afford.

It was five-thirty. He had another half-hour before he met Hartmann and the old man Krause at the 'Jaegersbrunnen' which was just across the road. Von Kornfeld had a horror of being late. It was one part of his training that seemed to have survived the deluge, he thought to himself. He finished his cigarette, got up from the bed and went over to the window. Standing on the tips of his toes, he looked down at the square of concrete that was the yard. It was a long way down, and it would be easy. Just alter the balance a little and you would be over before you even knew you were falling…

At last it was time to go. He descended the five flights of stairs, hugging the wall in the darker parts. On the third floor he met Rosa Spielmann. She looked tired and very pale without the usual rouge. She must have found someone for the whole night, he thought. Perhaps someone from the Police Barracks. It had been pay day yesterday for them.

'Morgen Captain,' she said, wearily.

'Morgen, Fräulein Rosa,' he said.

He was always rather worried whether he should not give her the courtesy title of 'Frau' – she was well over forty. But, he decided, ladies in her profession probably preferred to be called 'Fräulein'.

On the first floor the door of the landlady's room flew open and he could smell the aroma of real bean coffee. Frau Meyer in a dirty flowered kimono waddled out in her best slippers.

The landlady ignored his greeting.

'Morgen, Frau Meyer. Schon Ausgeschlafen?'

'Was that that dirty line-walker I just heard?' she said. Frau Meyer was in the Party, although she owned property.

'No, Frau Meyer,' he lied. 'It was Herr Kulman emptying his slops.'

He didn't give her the chance to develop the conversation. He detested having to tell lies.

Von Kornfeld went out into the tiny yard,

smelling of white cabbage, past the low basket-work prams and bicycles into the street. It was already busy, in spite of the early hour: men in the dress of their trades; carpenters in black corduroys and sombrero; plumbers in their blue-and-white-striped linen jackets; painters in their white peaked caps – and all carrying dirty white rucksacks or battered imitation leather brief-cases.

Von Kornfeld halted and let a column of tired, unshaven young men go by on their way to the factory. Instinctively he looked up at it. Just slightly to the left outside the wall was the one remaining tower of the old castle. It was said that they were going to take that down, too, next month, and then there would be nothing left. He remembered how they'd all looked down from the tower as children and watched the lights of the town in the snow on winter's nights. It seemed a long time ago now. Besides, he thought, they're all dead now, anyway.

He pushed aside the felt curtain and went inside the 'Jaegersbrunnen'. It was crowded with working-men in peaked caps, having an early morning drink before they went on their shift. One or two of them nodded to him dourly. In the corner he saw Krause and Hartmann. He went over and shook hands.

'Morning, together,' he said.

'Morning, Mr von Kornfeld,' Krause said, smiling. 'How goes it?'

'It goes.'

'Morning, Kornfeld,' Hartmann said shortly. 'You're on time.'

'Of course.'

Veidt, the owner, shuffled over in his felt slippers, bottle of Korn and glass in his hand. 'Morgen,' he mumbled. ''N' Korn?'

Von Kornfeld slipped his hand in his pocket and counted his loose change quickly, without looking down. 'A Corn,' he said.

Hartmann laughed. 'How does it feel to be poor – Von Kornfeld,' he emphasized the 'Von'.

'It goes.'

A squad of Barracked People's Police marched by towards the factory, singing.

'Another fighting-for-freedom song,' Von Kornfeld said. 'They're always fighting for freedom.'

Krause raised himself slightly from his chair and peered through the small window. 'Fine young men,' he said sadly. 'Fine young men. Pity they aren't with us.'

'Think, old man!' Hartmann said sharply.

'What can one expect? Revolutions are no longer made by young men. It's old men with memories who make revolutions nowadays. Old men with memories,' he repeated the phrase disgustedly.

'Thou art not old, Hannes,' Krause said.

'Of course thou art not,' Von Kornfeld added, and for some reason he used the familiar form of address.

Hartmann looked at him for a moment. 'Since when have we herded swine together?' he asked coldly.

It was an insult, and Von Kornfeld went red. In the old days it would have been necessary to slap Hartmann lightly across the face and then let it happen. He remembered the Beer Evenings as a student and the fights. 'May I ask why you are fixing your eye on my lady companion?' A light slap from left to right with the glove and then the card: 'Philosophy Candidate von Kornfeld.' Of course it had been forbidden, but the university had been full of young men running around with their wounds covered with black paste that was supposed to make a good deep scar. The police always looked the other way, anyway. But that had been almost a quarter of a century ago, and he'd learnt a lot since then.

'I'm sorry, Hartmann,' he said quietly. 'I

can't be properly awake. Anyway' – he forced a smile – 'we've known each other long enough. I offer you the "thou" now. What about it, Hartmann?'

Hartmann shook his head vigorously. 'Nay, not with me, Kornfeld. I work with you in the lock and we're in this together, but it doesn't mean I have to like you. You and your kind never change. Often I ask myself why you're in this at all. And the only answer I get is that you want to be up there again,' he jerked his thumb in the direction of the factory and the one remaining tower. 'You want to be up there, playing the big noise again. We're in this together, but don't go trying to jump over the fence.'

'Hannes,' Krause said soothingly. 'Don't get so excited. There have been gentlemen in the Socialist parties before today. Think of Lassalle, and Bebel once said that–'

'Bebel! Social Democrats! Go mi an Land mit Sozialisten! All theory and promises and pay your party dues regular every month!' Hartmann sneered.

'Look,' Von Kornfeld said, interrupting him. 'A stranger.'

The three men stared at the man, who had pushed aside the curtain and stood peering about in the smoke, hands deep in the slit

42

pockets of a 'Joppe' – the three-quarter-length coat worn by farmers.

'Kennst du den, Ewald?' Hartmann asked the old man.

'No, Hannes. He's not from here.'

They watched the man go to the counter and order a drink. They couldn't hear what he'd ordered. But a few moments later Veidt brought him a little bottle of rum and a steaming glass of hot water.

'Rum grog,' Krause said, and they watched him dissolve the lump sugar in the hot water, poking at it with the glass rod, and then pour in the rum.

'That must be him,' Von Kornfeld said. 'Who else would order rum grog on a day like this, when it's already twenty-five degrees at six o'clock in the morning?'

'Art thou going, Hannes?' Krause asked.

Hartmann did not say anything, but watched the man at the counter a little longer. Then he got up, pulled his short leather jacket down at the back and went over. He tapped the man on the shoulder.

'Don't I know you from the Moabit in Berlin?' he asked.

Richard Burdon turned round and looked at him. This must be one of them, he decided.

'No, I've been in better prisons than that.'

'You from Berlin?'

'No, I'm from the north.'

Hartmann introduced himself, and they went over to the others.

Krause got to his feet and stretched out his hand.

'My name's Krause. A rare name, like Meyer and Schulze.'

Burdon smiled and took the big, heavy hand with the thick black-blood veins sticking out.

Von Kornfeld gave the suspicion of a bow. 'Von Kornfeld.'

'My name's Richard Burdon.'

'Bur-don.' Krause mouthed the name slowly and with difficulty. 'That is a strange name. Is it from the north?'

'Man, wake up!' Hartmann snapped. 'It is not a German name at all.' He turned to Burdon. 'You are not German?'

'No, I'm an – American.'

'An American?' Krause said. 'I thought you weren't from the north. Do you know that when they speak dialect in the north we can't understand them, and when we speak our dialect they can't understand–'

'Shut up!' Hartmann said. 'An American. What can we do with you? An Ami!' He

44

looked straight at Burdon. 'Ach, du Arsch-krampf!'

Ami: the name was an insult the way he said it, Richard thought, but he kept his temper. There were always people like Hartmann on this sort of thing.

'They sent me because I'm a specialist,' he said quietly. 'I know all about these things.'

'Do you think we don't?' Hartmann said angrily. 'Do you think you can teach us anything?'

'I think so. At least I'll try to.'

Suddenly Veidt shouted from the bar: 'Die Bullen kommen!'

The Police.

'Die Vopos!' Krause said. They bent their heads over their drinks.

The curtain was pushed aside and Wagner and Todt came in. They seemed tired, and Wagner's face was blue-black where he needed a shave. They looked as if they had just come off night duty. Wagner nodded to one or two of them cheerfully, but his nods were not answered. The two policemen went over to the bar and ordered drinks.

They stood, their backs to the bar, and drank Corn. Everywhere conversation had dropped to a murmur. Men began to finish their drinks with a swallow and leave. Hartmann picked up his canvas rucksack and slung it over his shoulder.

'Come on,' he said. 'Let's get out of here.'

The others rose, Burdon with them. The place was nearly empty when they went out.

Wagner nodded to Krause. 'Morgen Ewald. How goes it?'

'It goes.'

'Fine.'

They left and Wagner looked at Todt's indignant face.

'Na?' he said.

'So'n Schweinerei!' Todt cursed. 'Why don't we make an example of somebody, Comrade Captain?'

Wagner flicked his peaked cap to the back of his head.

'A man can't stand on one leg. Veidt, let's have another Corn.'

'I'll have a beer,' Todt said, a little sulkily.

'Beer. Beer's just water. Gives you lice in yer belly.'

The drinks came, and they touched glasses.

'So you want to make an example of somebody,' Wagner said, wiping a thin line of liquid off his lips with the back of his hand. 'How? For what? If a working-man wants to finish his drink and go when we come in what can we do about it?'

'But it's a deliberate insult to us, Comrade Captain,' Todt protested.

'Probably is, but there's nothing you and I can do about it unless we start going round arresting everybody. Veidt, give us another. Zum Abgewoehnen. To stop the habit.'

Veidt laughed politely and filled the glass again.

'No, it's no use trying to push your head through the wall, man. You'd be better employed using your eyes. Did you, for example, Comrade Lieutenant, see the man with Hartmann and Krause?'

Todt shook his head.

'Of course not. Well, he's a stranger here, and in queer company. Now what about you trying to find out who he is, eh, Comrade Lieutenant?'

Wagner threw back his head and downed the Corn, and Todt could see the jagged dull purple weal round his neck where they had hanged him that time at Sachsenhausen. It made him shudder a little, and yet the feeling was in some way pleasurable.

CHAPTER FOUR

They were walking past the Ernst Thael-
mann Kaserne – the barracks of the People's
Police – when Hartmann pressed the muscle
of Burdon's arm hard. 'Look over there,' he
said, 'but keep walking.'

Richard Burdon looked through the
wooden railing at the open space dotted with
a few black crosses from the war. 'A cemetery,' he said.

'Yes,' Hartmann said, 'a cemetery. And
there' – he pointed to two Russian-style
graves, with photographs of the dead in glass
jars on the top of the mounts. 'How many do
you see?'

'Two.'

'Yes, two. We killed them this month, and
there's another one they haven't found yet.
We don't need specialists, you see. We're
specialists ourselves.'

They walked on in silence; Hartmann in
triumph and Von Kornfeld and Krause in
embarrassment. They came to the end of
the lane and stopped.

'Thou'lt see our Ami's all right, Ewald?' Hartmann said to Krause.

Krause nodded and they shook hands. Hartman didn't offer to shake hands with Richard Burdon and turned away while Von Kornfeld said goodbye.

'I'm sorry that it's like this, Mr Burdon,' Von Kornfeld said, 'but it's difficult for him. He believes in no one but his own kind' – he shrugged his shoulders hopelessly – 'and there is no one of his own kind on our side.'

'Come on,' Hartmann said roughly. 'Schulze geht die Weande hoch – Schulze'll go up the walls if we're much later!'

'Goodbye then, Mr Burdon,' Von Kornfeld said hastily. 'We'll be seeing you soon.'

Burdon and Krause watched them go back towards the town: Hartmann short and squat, his gait brisk and full of confidence; Von Kornfeld tall and thin, his shoulders slightly stooped and the hand that grasped the shoulder-strap of his rucksack thin and fine, unlike the broad sausage fingers of the other two, flattened and thickened by years of grasping and turning and forcing and twisting.

'Hartmann doesn't like me very much,' Burdon said suddenly, turning to the old man.

Krause was embarrassed. Burdon could feel that the man liked him. 'It's not that, Mr Burdon. He is a very queer man. He was in the Party ever since he was a boy. When Archer came in 1933 he went underground. For twelve years he was always fighting against them. Pamphlets from the roof of the cinema when the crowds were coming out. Copies of the "Red Flag" inside the local paper. Writing on the wall. Not the big things – just little ones, and all on his own. And always waiting for the day when they would come. And when they did come, what did they do? They raped and murdered and they put him inside with the men he'd been fighting against. It was all the same to them – red or brown, they were all German-ski. All he'd believed in for twenty-four years went in twenty-four hours one day in May 1945. So now he has nothing left but hate. That he learnt well. How to hate.'

Burdon listened to the old man and realized again how good simple people were in their assessments. He could never have summed up Hartmann's character like that even if he'd known him a hundred years. For him there would have been too many side-turnings and complications.

'And Von Kornfeld,' he asked. 'Who's he?

He's not a working-man, is he?'

'Von Kornfeld a working-man?' The old man laughed at the idea. But there was nothing bitter about the laughter. It was just that Burdon had said something funny. 'No, Von Kornfelds were the big Gutsherren – the landowners – around here. Where the factory is now, that's where they had their home. Now there's only the tower left. The family were all killed in the war. Africa, France, Russia – everywhere Archer sent them. They all died the "Heroes' death for the Fatherland".' He grinned a little at the thought, for some reason of his own, showing large yellow teeth under his graying toothbrush of a moustache. 'Except this one, of course. He came back last year from Ivan. Five years they had him. We thought he'd go over the border to the West like the rest of his kind, but he didn't. He stayed, and now he works in the lock like me and Hartmann. Couldn't say why.'

They had walked a long way up the narrow, dusty road. It was hot for the time of day and Richard's shirt was sticking to the small of his back. He opened his Joppe and cursed the man in the Stores who had picked this outfit for him. He breathed out heavily.

51

'Is it far to where we're going?' he asked.

The old man smiled, his black eyes almost losing themselves in the wrinkles. 'You're not used to walking, eh, Mr American? You always ride in your big car – in your Ford?' he added hastily, and then smiled, pleased with himself that he had remembered the name.

'Ye, we always ride in our big cars – in our big Fords.'

The old man nodded his head gravely, as if acknowledging the fact. Then he said, 'Is it true that the American worker rides to work in a big car? I have read this, but I do not quite believe. For instance, I am a brick-layer – I was a bricklayer – would I ride to work in such a car?'

'Yes, if you kept up your instalments,' Burdon said.

The old man frowned. 'Instalments! I do not like instalments; but still it is impressive. But in my trade clothes get dirty – you know, from the bricks. Would I still be allowed to drive a car?'

'Of course, if you keep up the instalments.'

'You see,' the old man explained, 'ever since I was a young man and joined the Party I have tried to learn. I have read and read and put things down in my book. How many people there are in China. Who was Voltaire. How many people in America have a car. Did you know that everyone in five has a car over there?' He looked at Burdon a little worried, in case he should be offended at the statistic from his own country.

'That is very interesting,' Burdon said.

'You see,' the old man said proudly, 'even a gentleman like yourself can learn from a man like me. I am an old man, but still I learn. I can speak with the unlearned workers about things that interest them and I can speak with cultured gentlemen like yourself. When one has learnt, the world is good and no longer frightening. Are you of this opinion too?'

But Burdon had no time to answer. Behind them came the rattle of a truck, jolting along the narrow, rutted road. Burdon pressed the old man on to the grass verge.

A police truck, with a guard, rifle slung over his shoulder, clinging grimly to the back of the cab, passed them, enveloping them in a cloud of dust. Through the laths in the back they could see something long and thin, wrapped up in a grey army blanket, which jolted up and down every time the truck went over a bump.

The old man walked along the road again,

avoiding Burdon's eye. 'From the factory,' he said after a time. 'Another one from that damned, damned factory...'

2

A woman was busy in the big garden when they turned in at the gate. She was small and plump. The backs of her bare legs were speckled green and blue with varicose veins. She wore the heelless wooden slippers of the peasants, her feet covered in thick grey woollen men's socks. Krause stopped.

'He's here, Mother,' he said.

The woman straightened up and shaded her eyes with her hand, although the sun was not strong, in spite of the heat. Her face was hard, brown and lined like a man's, but her eyes were soft, liquid and hurt. They were the eyes of a woman. She came over to the garden gate, wiped her calloused hand on her blue apron and shook his hand.

'Very pleasant,' she said.

'Very pleasant,' he repeated the intro-duction.

The old man was suddenly happy. 'The chickens laid this morning. We'll have eggs, Mütti.'

'Mütti,' she said scornfully, 'thy food is ready for thee. Tell Stine to make your coffee when she comes back from the berries.' She returned to her hoeing.

The old man waited a moment for her to say something else, but when she didn't he took Burdon by the arm and led him to the house.

It was ugly and old. It was built of red brick that the years had failed to mature. The walls were splashed with long streaks of bird-lime and under the eaves still hung the long, dried, yellow leaves of the remains of the previous year's tobacco crop.

The old man stopped at the step, pulled off his battered shoes without undoing the laces, and put on a pair of the heelless wooden slippers that stood there. They went into the kitchen.

The kitchen was big, but most of the room was taken up by a large home-made table covered with a threadbare American cloth, the pattern of which had almost vanished from constant rubbing down. A wooden bench ran the length of one wall, and in the opposite corner stood the large white fire-oven, the dented stove-pipe, disappearing into a hole in the wall just below the roof. Next to it on a bench stood three enamel buckets of water. That and three battered chairs completed the furniture.

Burdon looked at the yellowed newspaper photographs of the Social Democrat leaders pinned to the unpainted wall: Schumacher leaning heavily on his secretary; Carlo Schmidt, plump and clever; Ollenhauer, dull and phlegmatic.

He looked at the old man. Krause was waiting for him to say something.

'Isn't it dangerous to have them there?' he asked.

'Yes. If the Vopos came I would have to sit. You know.' He put his fingers outstretched in front of his eyes to emphasize his meaning. 'But that doesn't matter. I'm old now, anyway. For twelve years I was frightened, Mr Burdon. I was frightened for myself, for my wife, for my children. It's hard to be brave when you have a family. I tore up my party book. I sent my children to their schools. I went to work for them, and my wife paid their Winter Help. I became their man. I understand now that this is no good. To conform only makes the fear grow greater. Now I am open in my opposition to them and I am no longer afraid' – he smiled – 'or – at least, not always.'

The old man went into the little room next

to the kitchen, which was the pantry, and fetched boards and a big plate of sliced sausage. He gave Burdon a board and a knife and then, hugging the black loaf to his chest, he cut off several thick slices, cutting towards himself and lifting the slice upwards each time just before the blade reached his chest. Burdon made himself a sandwich, using the board as a plate like the old man.

Suddenly, with a gesture of annoyance, as if he had forgotten something, the old man got up and went into the little room again. He reappeared, holding a bottle and two glasses, nipped together between his big fingers. The bottle had no label. He poured out a glass and handed it to Burdon.

They touched glasses. 'Zum Wohle,' the old man said.

It took Burdon's breath away. 'What is it?' he asked.

'It's potato schnaps. We make it ourselves. They say it does things to you up here.' He touched his temple with his finger.

Burdon laughed. 'Perhaps that is good. It is not good to think too much – or too clearly.'

They had a few more drinks and more sausage and bread, the old man picking up with a moistened forefinger every crumb he lost from the board.

After a while the door opened and the girl came in. In her hand she had a milk-can full of some kind of dark red berries. Her hands were stained and scratched. She stopped when he saw Burdon, but the old man waved her to come in.

'Stine,' he said, taking hold of her hand, as if she would otherwise run away, 'this is the gentleman we have been waiting for.'

Burdon got to his feet and held out his hand. She transferred her can from one hand to the other.

'My hands are dirty,' she said and went red. She stretched out her little finger and they hooked little fingers together.

'My name's Richard Burdon.'

'Richard Bur-don.' She said the name slowly, pronouncing the Richard harder in the German fashion, and emphasizing the Burdon falsely.

'My name's Stine,' she said, suddenly looking down at her feet, as if she had said something she shouldn't have.

'Make some coffee for us, Stine,' the old man said.

'Yes, Father.' She put the can down on the window-sill. 'Shall I take the beans?'

'Naturally. We can't offer the gentleman

58

ersatz. And make it strong. No *pluie* today.'

The girl nodded and went about her task. She took the rings off the oven with the curved end of the poker, spread a handful of brushwood on the embers and blew hard until they began to crackle and burn. Then she replaced the rings and put the blackened kettle on. She sat down and began to grind the beans, the square grinder gripped firmly between her knees.

He watched her closely. She must be about eighteen or nineteen, he decided. She had a good face, strong and dark in the Central European manner, dark brown hair, bleached tawny by the sun at the front, a longish nose and a row of even, white teeth.

She sensed him watching her and she went red again. He tried to concentrate on the food, but found himself looking at her again. It was one of the rules he had for this sort of thing – don't get involved with their women, unless they're willing and there'll be no complications. And yet he couldn't take his eyes off her.

She got up to put the drawer full of coffee in the pot, and he watched her neat walk and the long thighs outlined against the thin material of her dress. And then the old man was asking something and he had to take his eyes from her.

The old man built up his question slowly and logically, like a man who had been in many arguments.

'You are an American?'

'Yes.'

'And you have been sent to help us?'

'Yes.'

'But you don't do this of your own accord?'

'No.'

'You come from an organization – an American organization?'

'Yes.'

'And possibly if we make the revolt we shall have their help: the help of this American organisation?'

Richard Burdon looked at the old man's face. It was an innocent face for an old man such as he was. He hesitated. The first lie was always a little difficult. How many times in the last ten years had it started like this, making pledges to innocent, hopeful faces – pledges that were no pledges. And when the time came for the pledges to be redeemed – well, he'd never been there when that time came round.

He hesitated. 'Yes, if you make the revolt and it looks like succeeding – having a majority behind it – it is possible that the Americans will come.'

He caught the girl looking at him, and he bent his head quickly over the food.

Then the coffee was ready, and the girl poured it out through the sieve and shouted for her mother through the open window.

The woman came in, sat down and began drinking her coffee without a word. Richard Burdon waited a moment, then took out his cigarettes and offered one to the old man. He smiled when he recognized the brand.

'Old Juno,' he said. 'It's many years since I last saw these. Look, Mother.' He held out the cigarette for her to see. 'A cigarette from the other side. Old Juno.'

His wife pushed the cigarette away and continued drinking her coffee. The old man lit his cigarette, puzzled.

'When the day comes, Mother,' he said after a while, 'the Americans will come–'

The woman put down her cup violently, spilling some of her coffee in the saucer. 'I don't want to hear anything about thy revolt or thy Americans! Nothing! Dost thou hear?'

'But why, Mother?' the old man protested. 'Then we'll be free again. Free for the first time for nearly twenty years. Isn't that important?'

'Free! What's that to me? What good is that if one is dead?' She turned to look at Richard. 'Look at my hands, Mr American.' She held up her creased, hard brown hands with the thumb split up to the knuckle from some old accident. 'Those are worker's hands. They worked under Hindenburg. They worked under Archer. They're working now! Whoever's up there, the worker has to work; it doesn't make any difference.' She turned to the old man again. 'All my life I've heard men talk like that. My father, thou, my son. Always politics. Politics, politics! And what has come of it? Nothing except fighting. So don't tell me about revolts. If thou want'st to be killed, go, but don't expect me to be happy about it!'

'But Mother,' the old man protested, but his wife bent her head over her coffee, and did not speak again.

3

Richard Burdon stood and smoked a last cigarette before going to bed. He had spent the day getting to know the layout of the town and the general situation. As far as he knew, it would be easy, except perhaps for

Hartmann. Hartmann might turn out a stumbling-block. He thought about it for a time, and then decided that he couldn't get any further that day. He relaxed and breathed in the night air.

Behind him stood the little town and, on the hill, the factory with its strange new-age silhouette illuminated by the arc lamps. Even at that distance he could hear the throb of its machinery, like the heart-beat of the little town. But now he was no longer interested in the factory or the little town. He stared at the light black of the sky just above the darker mass of the pine-forest. He felt somehow that behind its black façade there was a life, waiting and watching; watching him. Waiting for him to make the next move.

He dropped his cigarette into the sandy gravel and stamped on the glowing end, grinding it well into the dirt, using more energy than was necessary for some reason that he couldn't think of.

Okay. The set-up was this. He was here 'on a job': a job, pure and simple, like any other job. He was here for the money. It was a pity about them. They were probably nice people. But what the hell? If it didn't come this year it came the next. You all got it in the end so what the hell?

He was about to go in when he heard footsteps in the gravel. He turned and the footsteps stopped. He crouched, and then he saw that it was the girl.

'Come closer, Stine,' he said softly.

The girl came forward slowly. He could smell her fresh soap smell on the clear, sharp air.

'I was going to lock up the animals,' she said.

'How old art thou?' he asked quietly.

'I shall be eighteen.'

'That is very old. No pig will be that old.'

'I am a woman,' she answered quickly.

'Then why dost thou allow me to call thee "thou"? Tell me that?'

He felt her warm and embarrassed in the darkness. She did not answer.

'Dost thou like me?' he asked, and felt for and took her hand. She did not withdraw it. 'Why are thou silent?'

'I am ashamed of myself a little.'

She looked up at him, and he could see the straight silhouette of her chin against the night sky.

'I appear foolish to thee, yes? I am a girl from the land. From a place behind the moon. And thou hast undoubtedly lived in a big city in America and hast driven in a big car – in a Ford without doubt, like my father says.' She pronounced the 'd' of 'Ford' like a 't'.

'It is possible.' He took her other hand in his. 'But thou art not foolish to me.'

'No.'

Suddenly, and he realized how stupid he was being as he did it, he drew her towards him and kissed her. It was clumsy, and their teeth bumped together, and yet it was good and like times a long time ago. He could feel her heart beating wildly close to him. The muscles of his body grew tight, and he seemed to grow light and swell. He released her.

'Thou art very young, little one,' he said. 'Think. I am twice as old.'

'It is not important,' she said quietly.

He laughed, but there was no happiness in it. 'It is. It is. Hast thou ever drunk the milk straight from the teat in the morning, when the grass is still wet and the milk is young?'

'Yes, many times.'

'It is the difference between that and when one gets the milk in bottles every morning on one's doorstep. And the milk is cool and clean and safe. And you get it, always the same with never a change, every morning of

65

every day. That is the difference.'

'I do not agree with thee,' she said seriously after a moment's thought.

He laughed and, putting his hands on her shoulders, turned her round.

'Go now. I am tired. Go and lock up thy animals. It is late.'

'It is late,' she said and hesitated.

'Good night, Stine,' he said, almost angrily. Then gently. 'Sleep well. Dream sweet.'

'Good night, Richard. And I do not agree with thee.' And she ran off into the darkness...

CHAPTER FIVE

On the evening of the next day there was a meeting held in the 'gute Stube' – the good room – of the Krause house.

Outside, the sky was still full of the molten thunderclouds, and the room was very hot, but, in spite of the heat, the stove had been lit so that the beer could be warmed in the pot of water on top of it. Krause handed round glasses of his homemade schnaps. In the ruddy glow from the open trap of the stove, which threw great moving shadows on the painted walls, Richard Burdon looked at the faces of the men who had come. They were patient, red, freshly-shaven working-men's faces. They looked like the faces of men who should be sitting at home in their stockinged feet, evening paper in one hand and cup of coffee in the other, instead of planning revolutions.

Hartmann got to his feet and rapped his glass noisily. One or two of the men laughed uncertainly; not used to Hartmann in this role. Then they were quiet. But Hartmann did not begin at once. Instead he looked slowly round at each face, as if he were trying to fix it in his mind. It was an old trick. The men tried to stare him out for a moment and then they dropped their eyes, a little embarrassed. Richard wondered at what party school he had learnt that trick. Then he began:

'Comrades, first of all, I should like to introduce you to someone from over there. This is Mr Burdon. He is an American, who has come to help us.'

The eyes which had been giving him curious half-glances all the time could now look at him openly without disrespect.

'And then,' Hartmann went on, 'the main thing. We have the day now. The seventeenth of the month. The seventeenth of June.'

'The seventeenth of June,' they repeated the words after him.

'On that day, Comrades, there will be risings all over the Zone. We'll make an end with the Grotewohl swine that day.' His face twisted in anger. 'When I see those garden dwarfs, the food falls out of my face.'

'They're still Germans, Hannes,' somebody said softly.

'Germans! No, they're pigs eating their own dirt! But that's not important at the

68

moment. Main thing is, it's going to happen.' He paused and let his words have an effect. 'It's going to happen.' Richard could see that he was having difficulty in controling his excitement. 'And then we'll have rid of the whole heap of them. Kind und Kegel. All of 'em.

'I thought we might have done it ourselves, but the big shots in the organization seem to think different. From Ewald here,' he nodded at the old man, 'I learn that the Americans will come if we make a success of this thing. Now what do we mean by success? By success, I should say is meant that we make enough trouble for two or three days to show the world that we mean business. Then the Americans will come. What do you lot say?'

'I agree, Hannes.'

'Me too.'

'Yes, that's it,' they said seriously, like men who had thought about it for a long time.

'Schön. But how are we to do it? On account of the Vopo barracks in town, I do not think we can fight there. There would be nearly as many Vopos as us. If we started anything there more of us would go hop than there is Meyers in ten Berlin telephone books. And even if there wasn't a police barracks in town I wouldn't fight there.

There's no position to hold, no place to fight from there. They'd make firewood out of us in twenty-four hours.

'No, the ideal place is the factory.'

Richard Burdon looked up quickly.

'Once we're in there, they won't get us out in a hurry. Neither the Vopos, nor Ivan. Cliffs on three sides to give 'em sore arses when we kick 'em down, and only one road to get at us. And you know as well as I do that they're not going to use artillery or bombs on their beautiful factory. So what it boils down to is this. It'll be man against man, and we'll be in the superior position. In that factory we could easily stick it out for a week if necessary – and the Amis'll be here before then.

'Now how do we go about it? It would be simpler if we all worked in the factory, but we don't. It would be just another lock-out and a little extra. But it isn't. Let's look at it systematic. Who's in the factory? One – Ivan and the Vopos. Guard duty and patrolling. How many? Twelve men at the gate and ten with dogs inside on patrol. Who else? The technicians. All party members with stamped-up party cards and *Das Kapital* on their bookshelves,' Hartmann said bitterly. 'And then there's us – the boilermen and frig-ups from the town. The so-called unskilled labour. That's the situation. What do we do about it?'

He paused and took a drink of the potato schnaps that Krause handed him.

'This. At six o'clock on the morning of the seventeenth, the night shift will leave for their barracks at Melen, four miles from here. But the day shift of technicians will not appear, nor will the conscripts. At five minutes past six the only workers in the factory will be our lot – boilermen and the like – the frig-ups. At ten minutes past six or thereabout the factory will phone Melen to inquire where the technicians are. They will receive the answer that they are on their way. They will do the same at the conscripts' barracks and receive the same answer. Both answers will be given by us – and both will be fake. For at exactly five-forty-five the conscripts will start a little escape, helped by ourselves. At five-fifty the technicians' truck from Melen will run over a mine – Party cards and all. At six-fifteen a truck like that from Melen will drive up to the gates of the factory.' He paused for a moment and then said simply, 'We'll be in that truck. From the inside the boilermen will sort them out, and we'll do the rest from outside. At exactly the same time we drive up, several of us will start sniping the Vopo barracks to keep them with their snouts in the dirt for a bit at least.' He swallowed dryly. 'Somebody give me some beer.'

He was handed a bottle of the warm beer and drank it hastily, his Adam's apple riding up and down his neck jerkily.

The eyes of his audience were shining. 'Man, Hartmann,' they said. 'Thou hast truly a head.'

'It is well thought-out.'

Hartmann allowed himself a smile and then glanced over at Richard. 'I'm a specialist in these things.' He turned to the others again.

'Das kriegen wir für 'n Appel un n' Ei! We're getting the place for an apple and egg.'

'Ay, for an apple and an egg,' they said.

They relaxed and lit short pipes or the strong working-men's cigars. Hartmann looked annoyed, but he gave them a few moments. Then he started again:

'Good. But we need rifles and ammunition to do it. You, Ami, what can you offer us?'

The others looked at Hartmann because of his use of the word 'Ami'. It wasn't such a bad word. It could even sound funny; but not the way Hartmann said it.

Richard decided to ignore it again. 'I can tell you that in two days you'll get rifles and two M.G.s for your use from over there. There'll be explosive too.'

'Explosive,' Hartmann said quickly. 'For what do we need explosive?'

Richard Burdon ignored the question. 'I have something to say, please. I do not agree that the factory should be held. I am of the opinion that we should blow it up – like we should the police barracks too. For this reason I have had the explosive sent. I suggest that we should not fight in the town, nor in the factory – but in the woods. Let the police come for us there. There every man of us will be worth three of them–'

Hartmann interrupted him angrily. 'Revolutions are not fought in the woods; they are fought in the towns, Ami! So we go in the woods and what happens? They will put a circle round us then cut us in half, in quarters, and we'll die in ones and twos at their pleasure. No, that's not for me, Mr American.'

'But we can't stand against regular troops,' Richard protested. Hartman was right, of course, but he must get them out of that factory. He must. Get them in the woods and then – well, if things didn't work out, they could always sneak back home.

Hartmann ignored him. 'Wollen wir abstimmen? Let's take a vote on it.' He nodded at the man nearest to him.

'Woods or factory?'

'Factory,' came the answer.

'Schmidt?'

'Factory.'

'Fein?'

'Factory.'

'Ewald?'

'Factory.'

'And the gallant captain – Kornfeld.' He looked at Von Kornfeld. 'Permission to speak sitting down?' he added quickly. It was supposed to be a joke, but nobody laughed.

Von Kornfeld hesitated.

'Hop, hop, out with the dung!' Hartmann urged.

Von Kornfeld flushed a little. 'Well, I think I agree with you, Mr Hartmann. If this was a long-term operation I should say, as a former soldier, that the woods would be better. But this is not the case, therefore I say – the factory.'

'Thank you, Mr Captain,' Hartmann said with mock courtesy.

'But what if the Vopos seize your wives and children and use them as hostages?' Richard Burdon said quickly. 'Then they would use–'

But he did not finish his sentence. The door flew open and Stine stood there, her brown face suddenly very white.

'Father,' she said. 'Quick! It's Dieter. He's hurt!'

The old man pushed by Hartmann and out of the door. A minute later he was back, supporting a young man in the uniform of the People's Police. The policeman's bright yellow hair was matted and covered with dirt, his trousers were wet up to the thighs, as if he had waded through deep water, and his right sleeve was holed high up on the arm, wet and dark red.

Hartman's eyes blazed. He pushed back his chair and went to the boy.

'Where have you come from?' he demanded.

'Can't you see he's hurt, Mr Hartmann?' Stine said.

Hartmann ignored her. 'Where?' he shouted.

'Salzwedel,' the boy said weakly, his lips scummed and cracked. 'I went over the hill the night before last.'

'Go on. Out with it, man!'

'I walked all last night and hid during the day.'

'And where did you get this from?' Hartmann shouted and tapped the policeman's sleeve.

The boy went pale and swayed a little. Stine put her arm round him.

'The first night. The Gendarmerie caught me.'

'And then you led them to us, eh?' Hartmann snapped.

'No, no,' the boy protested weakly and leaned against his father.

'Right. Listen, everybody. Get off quick. Just in case.'

Men got to their feet quickly, neglecting to finish their drinks, and pushed their way to the door. Hartmann turned to the old man.

'Ewald, thou. Take thy son and hide him quick.'

'But he is hurt badly, Hannes, and he needs a doctor.'

'A doctor! Where? Every doctor within fifty kilometers of here would denounce him as soon as he stuck his snout in the surgery. No, Ewald, thou canst smear thy doctors in thy hair. Perhaps it will give thee locks.' He put on his peaked cap. 'Thou'lt have to look after him the best thou canst. But hide him. Hide him quick!' He finished his drink and with a glance at the boy, went.

The boy slumped heavily into a chair and his head fell on his chest. Richard Burdon looked at him for a moment. Nobody moved. He got up and went over. With his pocket knife he slit the sleeve of the boy's jacket, then he did the same with the grey flannel shirt.

'Stine,' he ordered. 'Give me the alcohol.'

The old man looked surprised that Richard has used the familiar form of address, but he didn't say anything.

Richard poured out a glass for the boy and made him drink it. Then he splashed a little on his handkerchief and carefully began to wipe away the congealed blood from around the wound. The boy started and bit his lip. Richard dropped the handkerchief on the floor and dipped the blade of his knife in the alcohol. Satisfied with it, he inserted it very carefully into the wound. Gingerly he felt for the bullet. He found it and the boy fainted.

After a moment Richard straightened up, wiped his knife and had a drink himself. He looked down at the boy's white face, as he lay there in the chair.

'I think it is necessary to take out the bullet. I have found it where it should not be. But it is not too deep.'

'But we have nothing,' the old man said helplessly, and spread out his hands, palms upwards.

'And the pain – the pain,' his wife said.

Richard Burdon put his hands deep in his pockets and looked at them. Why get involved? What was it to him? A young man in pain. Many young men suffered pain, and many more would do. It was the way of things.

'And thou, Richard,' the girl said, looking up at him. 'It will hurt? We have nothing that will deaden the pain.'

Richard took his hands out of his pockets and brought out a little white bottle. He poured the tablets it contained into the palm of his hand. 'These will help,' he said. 'But they are not enough. Stine, hast thou "Koelnisch Wasser" or such?'

'Yes, yes, I have. I have it still from my Name's Day. Why dost thou ask?'

'Bring it, please, and if thou hast an atomizer bring that too.'

'An atomizer. What is that?'

He explained.

She shook her head. 'No, we have not one

78

of those.'

'We have,' her mother said.

'Get it,' Richard said, 'and bring them back quick. I'll need someone to hold him.'

While they were gone he dissolved six tablets in alcohol and forced the boy to drink the mixture. Then they were back. They had filled the spray with the eau-de-Cologne. Richard tried it in the air while they looked on.

'I've given him the tablets,' he explained. 'This should help to deaden the pain too. It freezes to some extent. But not completely, of course.'

He began to spray the wound with the perfume. The boy shivered and goose-flesh prickled his right cheek.

'What are you going to do?' he asked.

Nobody answered. Richard began to clean his knife with alcohol again. The boy sat up quickly.

'It is impossible,' the old man said suddenly, his eyes wide-opened, focused on the knife. 'It is impossible. There will be too much pain.'

'Must the bullet really be taken out?' the old man's wife asked, her voice completely controlled.

'Yes, it must. If we must hide him without

the attention, his arm will – how does one say? – will die before long. They will have to take it off.'

The boy reached forward and clasped the wrist of his injured arm tenderly, as if to assure himself that it was still there.

'Good,' the woman said. She walked over and held his shoulder. Then she looked at her husband. 'Take his other shoulder, man. Stine, help the American.'

The boy looked from one to the other of them, his eyes full of pain and terror. 'Give me a drink, please,' he said thickly.

'We haven't time now,' Richard said, finishing the cleaning of his knife. 'Otherwise the effect of the perfume will wear off.'

He nodded to the old man and his wife and they took a firm grip. He brought up his knife. The boy groaned and looked away.

He brought the knife close to the opening of the wound. It was bleeding slightly where he had cleaned it. He felt his muscles go hard. It was difficult. He felt the sweat forming on his forehead. Then he did it – violently. The boy screamed and his head dropped on his chest.

The woman went very white under her tan, but she did not relax her hold. Quickly Richard began to cut into the remaining flesh around the wound, the fresh blood pouring out over his hand and obscuring everything in a moment. He worked rapidly and by touch, praying the whole time that he wouldn't hit one of the main arteries. Between his fingers the blood was beginning to congeal. His shirt was sticking damply to the small of his back.

'Quick,' he said to Stine, 'give me a damp cloth!' He did not take his eyes off the boy. He began to stir, and Richard pressed a little harder into the flesh and the boy fainted again. It was better that way.

Stine gave him the handkerchief. He plugged the wound, drew the cloth out quickly and caught a glimpse of the bullet before the wound flooded with blood again. It was nearly out. He took the knife up again and began to cut. The boy looked bad. His face was deadly white and his lips were blue.

And then it was out. He reached in a finger and pulled it out, covered with blood. He dropped it on the floor and straightened his back for a moment.

'Cloths – anything to stop the blood,' he said.

They handed him handkerchiefs, rags and, dipping them in the alcohol, he plugged in the wound. The blood flow slackened

81

a little, but not enough. Suddenly he was very angry. He couldn't remember the word for tourniquet. 'Tie a tight bandage round underneath the wound. Perhaps we'll be able to plug it better then,' he said.

He sat down heavily and let them do it. He was sweating all over. He had allowed himself to become involved. He was in now...

2

The house was empty except for the girl and himself. Her parents had gone with their son into one of the outhouses, where they would hide him for the night, taking turns to loosen the tourniquet until the bleeding stopped. It might take several hours.

Richard sat back in the chair and yawned.

'Thou art tired, Richard?' the girl said.

'Yes, such things make one tired.'

'Will he be all right?'

'He'll live. It's not the best way to get a bullet out, but he looks a strong boy.' He yawned again.

'Du bist ja so müde,' she said.

'It's immaterial. A few days and the whole thing will be over, and then I can sleep as long as I want.'

He saw immediately that he had said the wrong thing. He was awake at once. He put his arm round her and she shook it off angrily.

'Then thou wilt be gone – back to thy city and thy big auto – thy Ford.' This time she pronounced it correctly, as he had taught her. This she did in spite of her anger.

Richard laughed at her mention of the car, and it made her angrier.

'Do not laugh, ape!' she said, flushed. 'Good, I am from the country. I don't know about things. But don't laugh at me.'

'I didn't laugh at thee – but with thee,' he said gently.

'With me?'

'Yes, with thee.'

He put his arm round her again. She was soft and firm, close to him. He felt her tremble. And then he touched her and she did not object.

'Thou wilt not hurt me,' she whispered dryly. 'I know little about this.'

'Never?'

'No, never if it is what I think. Never.'

He slackened his grip, but she pressed herself closer to him.

'It is not that I am afraid,' she said softly; 'it is that I am ashamed at my ignorance.'

Richard smiled. 'Thou art young and I have known many women before. This is an obviousness. Eine Selbstverständlichkeit.'

He wanted to, and yet suddenly he was afraid. How could they do it without fear? He looked at her, waiting. He didn't want to, but he knew he would. He would do it. For her it would be the first time, and yet it would be the last. Once and never again.

'This is foolish,' he said. 'We don't know what will happen in a few days. Thou art young and do not understand these things.'

'I understand only this,' she said quietly. 'I am ready and want to – with thee. With thee, Richard.'

'Christ! Why can't it all be simple again?' he cursed in English. 'I should just take you. Whip up your skirts and pull your hands behind your back. And here I am thinking, worrying about pros and cons. Oh, what the hell!'

The girl looked puzzled, her forehead creased in a frown. 'What doest thou speak? I have not understood. Please what is it?'

Richard relaxed and attempted a smile. 'It is nothing. I am sorry. I was speaking English. When it becomes too much I sometimes do.'

'Thou art angry with me?' Her lips pouted

like those of a small child.

Richard laughed and pressed her hand. 'No, I'm not angry. I could never be angry with thee.' He kissed her, and it felt as if something had gone out of him. It took his breath away. This time it was he who trembled.

'No,' she whispered. 'No, not here.'

'Why?'

'I don't know. But not here.'

'Where, then?'

'Outside. The hill in the forest. Come.'

They got up. She took his hand and they went out of the room, leaving the door wide open behind them.

They walked quickly across the meadow behind the house, edged blue-green in the moonlight, through the gate and towards the spiked blackness of the forest. Then into it at a half-run, with the trees reaching out and trying to bar their way. They were running uphill and out of the forest, the long, wet grass lashing softly at their legs. And then they were together as one person...

Richard Burdon wriggled out of his jacket, without taking his arm from underneath her. She smiled in her sleep and moved closer to him. Gently as he could with one hand, he spread the jacket over her.

He looked at her while she slept. In sleep there was nothing in her face – just sweetness and calm. It was the face of innocence. Once he had had a face like that. Everybody had. But you didn't have it long. He remembered how the whores had told him he'd had that kind of face that year in Spain. But he didn't have it long. But then the next year most of them had been dead, anyway. So what did it matter?

He yawned and looked up at the sky. It was big and it frightened him a little. The sky was complicated, just as things had been complicated for him. Half an hour ago it had been simple. Thirty thousand dollars in a few days time in that small private Boston bank. A job of work and thirty thousand dollars. And then the secret house beneath the white cliffs. But now it had become complicated.

'Christ, man, think straight,' the tiny voice inside him said. 'You're kidding yourself. Act your age. There are girls like her anywhere if you go and look for them. In the small towns and villages all over Europe you'll find 'em. There's nothing special about her. Anyway, tomorrow it'll all be different. You'll be the same, but she'll be different. Aren't you just romanticizing the whole damn thing? Isn't it a bit of middle-class imagining? Isn't this how they expect war to be? A bit of danger and getting your eats in foreign places? An opportunity to get into kipp with a different woman from the one they usually get in with? Hadn't it always been like this – fear and the war and the shortage of time making everything seem more intense?'

And as he thought about these things, he knew that he just couldn't believe them.

He craned his neck to look at the luminous dial of his watch, and then looked away quickly before he had seen it. He mustn't worry about time now. But the sudden gesture awoke the girl. She woke completely and at once.

'Thou hast snored,' he said. He was interested to see her reaction.

'I did not,' she said promptly.

He smiled in the dark. He was glad that she reacted like that, without any simpering and self-accusation. He hated that fall-of-man act that some of them put on.

'We must go,' he said. 'It is time!' Under his breath he cursed, but it was too late. He had said it. Time. You just couldn't escape it.

She held him to her. 'Let us stay here a moment longer, please. It is important to me. I don't want to see people straightaway.'

'It was important for thee to come here,' he said. 'Why was this?'

She hesitated and looked down at the grass. He raised her chin in his hand. 'It is difficult to say. I think because – a couch, a room, a house. One day all these will disappear. The earth will stay. It is always there. A couch, a room, a house. They become dirty and broken and ruined, but every year the earth is green and new again. That is how I wanted it to be between us. I can look at this hill from now until the day I die and know – perhaps remember about us.' She was suddenly very embarrassed. 'I have said a great deal, haven't I?'

'But it is true what thou has said,' Richard said softly, and stroked her hair slowly. 'And it is in a way beautiful.'

And sad, too, the sentence ran on in his brain, but he did not say that.

'But if I come with thee, Richard,' she said thoughtfully, 'I will no longer be able to see the hill.'

'Come with me,' he said. 'How didst thou come to that idea? An innocent from the country would be of no use where I live. Thou canst not even drive in a Ford,' he pronounced the word as she did. 'Without this ability thou wouldn't be able to leave thy house.'

'Is this true?' she asked, half-believing, half-unbelieving. 'Must I be able to do this?'

He laughed out loud and ruffled her hair. 'Of course not, little one. Bei dir haben sie wohl eingebrochen! By thee they have broken in, eh?'

She laughed too and smoothed her hair down. 'Thou speakest good German.'

'I can do more. Listen, little sparrow. Thou hast air in they tooth, man! Thou hast a little bird which goes twirp-twirp! By thee it is too tight!'

'Enough, enough!' she cried, laughing. 'I am convinced. Thou hast more knowledge than I.'

'See. How much more thou will have to learn before thou canst go with me.'

'Yes. I must learn,' she said eagerly. 'I want to know all. And about thee, too. Where thou wast born. Much, much. And thou must teach me English. I speak Russian. We had to learn in the school. Once I got a Two. That is good…'

She stopped suddenly. High above the trees, in the thin air that lightly disturbed the tops of the pines, came the sound of the siren; loud and then faint again as the wind turned.

'The factory siren.'

She pressed herself close to him, and he felt her heart beating rapidly.

'What is the matter, little one?' he asked anxiously. 'It is only the siren.'

She did not say anything for a moment. 'It means a death when they sound the siren apart from the shift beginning and end. It is a signal for the wagon to come from the town to fetch the ... the dead one!'

He felt cold, and he could not prevent himself shivering. 'A louse ran over my liver,' he said, attempting a joke, but it failed.

'While we were–' She left the sentence unfinished.

'A man died,' he completed it for her, his voice toneless. 'A man died.'

'Richard, Richard,' she almost screamed. 'Thou must never leave me. Never! Please!' She clutched him, and he felt her nails bite into the thin material of his shirt and into his flesh. 'Please!'

'Yes, Stine. I promise. I shall never leave thee now. Never...'

CHAPTER SIX

Breakfast next morning was an awkward meal. No one spoke very much. They ate a great deal of the brown bread and sausage and chewed stolidly, their eyes fixed for the most part on the bare table.

Afterwards Stine and her father went out into the yard to clean it, the girl slaking the thick dust with a watering-can and the old man raking it smooth with a long, light-metal pronged rake.

In the kitchen Richard watched the old woman, as she placed chairs upside down on the table preparatory to waxing the floor. While she rubbed the wax into the floor-boards they talked.

'I should like to thank you, mister, for helping my son last night,' she said, rubbing in the hard, cold wax without any apparent effort.

'It was nothing. Anybody who knew a little about these things would have done it,' he said uneasily.

'I thank you all the same.' She continued

polishing mechanically. 'I am fifty, Mr American. I am an old woman. I've worked all my life and have nothing to show for it, you understand. Always there have been revolutions, inflations, leaders. All I want for myself is peace. I expect nothing more from the world now.' She dipped her rag in the polish. 'But for my children I don't want that. You understand.' She looked up at him with those brown liquid woman's eyes of hers. 'You understand. No trouble for my children.'

'Yes, I understand. I understand well.'

Later that morning Richard went over with the old man to the outhouse where they had hidden the son. He had a look at the arm, but did not take the bandage off. It wasn't worth the risk of having the thing start bleeding again. Except for a dusky red patch just beneath the bandage the arm looked all right, as far as he could see. Richard put his hand on the boy's forehead for a moment. It was hot, but a little fever was to be expected, he supposed.

'How goes it?' he asked.

'It goes,' the boy said, looking at him curiously. 'But it is stiff. Pretty stiff. It hurts a lot when I move it.'

'That is normal. It is to be expected.' He put the jacket over the boy's shoulder again and watched while the old man helped his son eat.

The boy had a different face from the old man and Stine. It was thin and long with a narrow, but full-lipped mouth; a mouth of controlled emotions. He had long, fair hair, badly cut, with a piece at the back which would never stick down, he supposed, as long as the boy lived. But it was the eyes which caught his attention. They were light blue and fierce and yet distant, full of that quality which only the Germans have a word for: *Innigkeit* – innerness.

'You are an American?' the boy said when he was finished with his food.

'Yes. An American.'

'You are different from how I imagined Americans to be. I had visualized them differently. You are not an Emigrant. No, you don't look like an Emigrant.'

Richard smiled to himself. Emigrant was the polite euphemism the Germans used for the people who had had to flee from the Nazis. He had expected something stronger from a member of the Communist youth, with their stock phrases.

'Yes, I am. I'm an Emigrant. An Emigrant

from England.'

'The gentleman was an Englishman before he was an American,' the old man explained.

'Ah, that is different,' the boy said. 'Yes, that is truly different.'

Richard remembered the lectures they had had on Political Science. Locke and Hume on the Social Contract. If you didn't like your country you had the right to dissolve the contract. It was as simple as that. It wasn't, really.

'You like America?' the boy was asking. 'Everybody there has big houses, big cars, big everything. They pay well in America.'

'It is possible. I am rarely in the country. I spend most of my time in Europe.'

'Why did you go, then?' the boy asked aggressively.

'Oh, I don't know. I have worked many years with Americans now. I decided I should become one too. I like the Americans on the whole.'

'They are afraid of us – the Amis,' the boy said proudly. 'They have the dollars – that is true. But we have our belief. We, the people will always win in the end.'

'It is perhaps as you say,' Richard said quietly.

People! He hated the very sound of the word. Most words that were supposed to mean anything he hated. He hated all these words which were supposed to make you feel good and do something. He hated these words as much as he could hate anything any more. He relaxed. A place in the sun in a country where he no longer felt involved. That's all he wanted now. A country where he could open the paper in the morning and not get angry or sad; where people could say the bitter things, the biased things, the stupid things and he could hear them without feeling moved one way or another.

'But why did you go over the hill, if you have the belief?' Richard asked pleasantly.

The boy was embarrassed for a moment. 'I have the belief. I still believe. Things always happen which are not pleasant. One cannot plane wood without spilling some sawdust. I have read of these things happening there, too, when it first started.'

'What things, son?' the old man asked softly.

The boy lowered his eyes. 'I prefer not to say, Pappa.'

The use of the child's word made Richard Burdon realize how young the old man's son was. He suddenly felt sorry for him. It was always hard. It had been hard for him that time when he got back from Spain.

'Tell me,' the old man persisted. 'Is this the reason why thou hast deserted? Is it?'

The boy nodded his head numbly.

'Then free away from the liver. If it is something that thou hast done, it can be forgiven, boy. Thou art still a child.'

'Don't give me that bourgeois morality!' the boy flared up. 'I want none of that! All my life I've heard it. Don't! Don't, don't! Be calm. Be moderate. It isn't that kind of a world, Pappa! Where can one be calm, good, moderate? Tell me that? In my prison we had a Social Democrat and he had been in there three years. And all that time he had never scratched the walls, never left his bed un-made, never forgot to empty his slops at the right time. Everything in his cell was tip-top. The walls clean as a new pin. No dates, no drawings, no messages, no nothing. And then they came and shot him – he was a saboteur, of course. And he never complained or cried or struggled like they do. He was like thou, Pappa. But he was shot all the same. He died and didn't even leave his name scratched on the cell-wall behind him. Who dost thou think, Pappa, will ever remember that he ever lived – for all his calmness, moderation and goodness? Tell me that, Pappa. Tell me that.'

Gently the old man placed his hand on his son's good shoulder. 'We were always like that, it is true,' he said as if he were thinking hard. 'Perhaps it was our fault. But please tell me–'

'Tell thee!' The boy laughed and the laughter hurt his arm and he winced. 'I'll tell thee. There were three of us and Schmidtkin – little Smith. Thou hast seen him once, Pappa.'

'Yes, I have seen him,' the old man said soberly. 'I have seen him.'

'Well, he was in charge. He's a section-leader now. We were patrolling the station at Salzwedel. It was a long afternoon and we were bored. Up and down. Up and down. Nothing doing. As boring as hell. Then old Schmidtkin says. "Listen, boys. I've got it up to here," and he puts his hand up to his mouth. "Bored as hell." We said we were as well. So he says. "Let's have a bit of fun." So we say. Good, we don't mind, as long as times goes quick. And he pulls this pamphlet out of his pocket that he'd got from some-where or other. One of those things that Bonn keeps smuggling in. "I picked this up the other day near the border," he says. "Well, what say I find this in somebody's luggage? See what happens. Just for the hell of it."

'I wasn't too keen. I didn't like playing about with that sort of thing. "I don't like it, Schmidtkin," I said. "I don't even like just joking with that sort of thing."

'"Au, come on," he says. "Don't be a misery." Yes, the others say. "Mitmachen. What the hell else can you do on a day like this, man?" They were all for it. They all knew Schmidtkin. He's a bit of lad that way. Yes, he's a bit of lad all right,' the boy laughed sourly at the thought.

'So I let myself be persuaded. It can't do any harm, I thought. And so we began to look for a likely character. One or two of the others pointed out what they thought would be likely types, but Schmidtkin wasn't having any. He was not right and he might give trouble and so on. Then he saw the type he was looking for. And we agreed with him. He was just right. Tall fellow with pince-nez and high stiff collar. Schmissesabre scars all down one side of his face. He looked like a retired schoolteacher or something like that. He was walking with a woman who looked like a horse.

'Schmidtkin looked at us and we looked at him.

'"Yes," he said.

'"Yes," we said.

'We went over and Schmidtkin stops them and touches his cap, very polite.

'"Excuse me, Comrade," he says. "I wonder if I could have a glance through your baggage?" Very meek and mild. We could have bust ourselves laughing – then. Anybody who heard Schmidtkin putting on this act, and knew him the way he really is, would have.

'The man with the pince-nez looked at his wife and she at him and then he says. 'I don't see why not ... er ... Comrade. I've nothing to hide.' All very upper-class like and a bit of hesitation over the "comrade".

'Schmidtkin touches the peak of his cap again. "Thank you, Comrade," he says.

'They open the cases and Schmidtkin bends down to examine them, while they pretend to be looking at the trains. You know, trying to make out that they were better than we were.

'Schmidtkin straightens up after finishing the first one.

'"All right," he says. "Won't be a minute now," and touches his cap.

'We were nearly peeing ourselves; this touching-his-cap business of his is nearly crippling us. Then he bends down again and finds it. No fuss. Very business-like. Very stern and a bit puzzled.

'"Hello! What have we here?" he says.

'The man looks at it and then at his wife as if he has just had a baby. "What's the matter?" he stutters.

'Schmidtkin plays stupid. He unfolds the paper. "I don't know, Comrade," he says, very serious-like, "but it looks very like a piece of sedition to me!"

'"Sedition?" the fellow with the pince-nez says. His missus goes white.

'"Yes."

'"Give me it, please!" He grabs at it and fumbles with his specs.

'Schmidtkin winks at us over their shoulders while they read it. We're biting our lips to keep ourselves from laughing at the look on their faces. It was like in the pictures.

'"I protest," the man said. "I protest. I've never seen this before."

'"That's what they all say, Comrade," Schmidtkin said very heavy. "Ain't it, boys?" He turns to us. We nod and say, that's right.

'"But my wife will tell you that I have not seen such a thing before. Wilma, isn't that true?"

'"Yes," she said, and she was looking at

him as if she had just found him with his pants down in a brothel. "Yes, Arnold."

""'Arnold.' Do yer hear that?", the bloke next to me whispered. "A proper Arnold, he is."

"'I'm afraid that's not good enough," Schmidtkin says, really very heavy this time. "I think this thing'll have to be looked into a little closer."

'The fellow with the pince-nez and his wife are properly scared now, and I'm trying to catch Schmidtkin's eye and tell him to pack in, but he won't let me.

'The bloke fixes his pince-nez and says, "I don't think you quite understand who I am, Comrade Officer. I am Privatdozent Arnold Kuster of the University of Jena, retired."

'Now that sort of thing doesn't go down well with old Schmidtkin. He can't hardly write himself and hates that la-di-da stuff. "And I don't think you understand who I am," he says, imitating the bloke.

"'I'm afraid I don't."

"'Well, I'm Professor of Pornography at the University of ... Timbuctoo," Schmidtkin says, and pulls off the bloke's pince-nez and puts them on his own nose. "Professor of Pornography I am..."

'Something happens to the man without

his specs. His face sort of loses form without them. Apart from that, you can see that he's blind as a bat.

'"Give me my spectacles," he says and reaches out his hand for them.

'"Say please, naughty boy," Schmidtkin shouts and jumps back out of his reach.

'The old woman moves forward, but Schmidtkin gives one of the boys a wink and he grabs her so that she can't move.

'"Here they are, Professor," Schmidtkin says and waves them under the bloke's nose.

'Of course when the man grabs for them, Schmidtkin puts them out of his reach. Well, this goes on for a bit until Schmidtkin gets tired of it. The man's almost in tears by this time and his missus is red in the face from struggling.

'"All right," Schmidtkin says and lays the specs down on the ground. "Here they are now. Don't start crying, Professor."

'The man clutches hold of Schmidtkin and then bends down and sweeps the ground for them, holding on to Schmidtkin's pants all the time. He's just about got them when Schmidtkin puts his heel on them and grinds them to splinters. The woman screams, breaks loose and slaps Schmidtkin across both cheeks left, right – right, left.

'"You swine!" she shouts. "Dirty swine! Tread on them like that! Swine! Pack! Proleten!"

'A little crowd has gathered, mostly "Young Pioneers" in uniform. Off to some rally, as usual.

'"Don't shout at me, you bourgeois sow!" he shouts back at her. "I'm a thousand times better than you!" He reaches out and gives the husband a bang in the guts so that he goes head-first in to the kids. The kids push him back. Everybody's pushing him now. The kids start to enjoy it. It's like a game for them. They start to push him from one to another.

'I go up to Schmidtkin. "Come on," I say. "Let's stop it. The bloke's had enough. It's gone far enough. We've had our bit of fun."

'"Hold thy trap!" he shouts at me. "I'll say when we stop!" I could see the white marks on his cheek where the woman had slapped him.

'Somebody kicked their case. The catch opened again and their clothes flew across the platform. One of the kids, a big blond lad, picked up a pair of red drawers like old women wear, with elastic at the knees. He waved them about and then put them on his head like some sort of hat. "Get me!" he shouted. "Get me! Ain't I nice?"

'Somebody kicked the other case open and everybody started pulling out the underwear and things; the old woman fighting them and trying to get the cases closed again.

'Then suddenly everybody remembered the man with the pince-nez. He was walking up the platform, falling over things all the time, trying to get away.

'"He's trying to do a bunk!" the kids all shouted. "He's trying to do a bunk!"

'And then the Berlin train came in – he didn't have an earthly.

'We all shouted, but he must have thought we were coming after him. I started to run after him, and that only made it worse. He must have thought I was chasing him. It made him move even quicker. And then he stumbled. I thought for a moment that he was going to keep his balance. But he didn't. Over he went, and that was it.' The boy puffed out his lips. 'I went over the hill that night when we got back to barracks. Just took off.'

Richard and the old man were silent. The old man looked embarrassed. 'Thou,' he said suddenly to the boy, licking his lips a little before speaking. 'It is in order now.

When thy arm is healed thou canst go back over the border.' He touched the boy hesitantly on the shoulder, as if he had never touched him before. 'Do not worry. It is in order now.'

'Ein Dreck in Ordnung!' the boy burst out. 'Thou art droll, Pappa! In order! Nothing's in order! Just because some bully causes a death. I run, desert my duty; and thou says all is in order! I come home and find it full of spies, saboteurs, reactionaries, and thou call'st that in order. Thou are droll, Pappa!'

He paused for breath, and the old man shook his head sadly. 'Thou dost not know what thou art saying. When thou art older, thou...'

'Older. It is always the same old argument. When I am older. This I know, Father, and I have always known it ever since I could remember. Thou and thy way of change is no good. It has no value. Always wait, wait and be patient. And in the end one is too old and patient to do anything at all. In five years we have done more than thy Social Democrats have done in fifty years.'

'Halt die Klappe. Hold thy trap!' the old man said, suddenly angry. 'I don't want to hear any more from thee. I shall go if thou sayest any more!'

'Well, go, then! For God's sake go!'

The old man hesitated. His wrinkled old face was flushed red. He looked at Richard. Richard took his arm and pulled him away gently.

'Come on,' he said. 'We have a lot to discuss about tonight.'

The old man let himself be led.

2

There were five or six of them in the dark with their trek carts. It was cold for June, and Richard Burdon turned the collar of his jacket up and listened to the wind in the trees. Hartmann repeated the orders again in a low voice.

'When the plane lands you'll make a line behind me and we'll unload systematic and quick. Get it?'

There was a low murmur of assent from the men.

'As soon as your carts are loaded you'll leave. Then off over there to Ewald.' He flashed his torch for a moment on the stooped figure of the old man standing next to a heap of manure. 'You'll pull your tarpaulins over the guns, and Ewald will cover the top with "mist" for you. Right?'

'Right.'

'After that you take the road I gave each of you and get back to town – but quick! Right?'

'Right.'

'Good. Then no more talking now.'

A few moments later they heard the faint, light sound of the plane.

'This must be it,' Hartmann whispered to Richard. 'Give the signal, Ami.'

Richard threw a quick glance at his watch and nodded. It must be the plane. He accepted Hartmann's torch and gave the signal: three short spots of light.

A second later came back an answering red flicker.

He turned on the torch and held it as a guiding light. And then the swirling blades were right above them and they were bathed in light from the helicopter's searchlight. Hartmann shouted something angrily, and a moment later the plane had landed rather heavily, rising off the ground again.

A hatch-cover was unlatched.

'Any of you gooks speak English?' a voice asked.

Richard turned his torch on a fat, pale face under a light tan forage cap, which was divided in two by earphones.

'Yes, I speak English,' he said.

'Okay, Mac. Get your boys on the beam. I've opened the cargo hatch.'

Richard translated for them, and they started unloading.

Richard had a last look at the pilot and then turned off his torch. Two hundred dollars a month and two hundred extra flying pay. Sold the Ford and buying a Porsche. Two eggs and ham for breakfast. Steak for dinner. Bourbon and crap in the club. Paris and Rome every month on the buckshee flights for flying personnel. A nudge in the ribs and a wink. 'Week-end out with the boys in gay Paree. Whoop it up a bit with the Frogs.' Some to Garmisch this winter! A fat Lieutenant in a plane in a German field on the wrong side of the border.

'Christ!' the Lieutenant cursed from his seat. 'Ain't you gooks finished yet? Listen you,' he said to Richard in the dark. 'You, the guy I just talked to. Tell them to hurry. Sie verstehen. Hurry. Schnell.' He repeated the words slowly, emphasizing each one as if he were talking to a very small child. 'Machen du schnell. Oder Russki bum, bum!'

Richard passed the message on.

'Hurry out with the dung!' Hartmann

shouted, not caring now. 'Our fat Ami has got the wind up!'

One cart was filled and squeaked its way rustily over the rough turf to where the old man stood with his manure. Richard could hear the pilot tapping nervously on his control panel. Suddenly he clicked on a dim light and started studying the map strapped to his knee, mumbling aloud the whole time.

'Been off the Corridor for – five minutes.' He was referring to the Air Corridor through Russian territory to Berlin. 'They'll have picked me and– Hey you. Du out there! Schnell machen! Russki here bald!'

Richard lost patience. 'Blow it out! Blow it out! The Russians won't get you this time, don't worry!'

'You American?' the pilot said, amazed. 'You don't sound like it much.'

'No, I'm the special kind – for export only. But perhaps you wouldn't know about that.'

'Eh?'

'Skip it!'

'I thought you was a Kraut, but will you tell these guys to make it snappy?'

'Don't sweat, G.I.'

'It's all right for you, brother, but if those Migs jump me I'm for the meat-wagon. I could use them at the moment like I could use a hole in the head!'

'It's a pity about you. I'll stamp your T.S. card some time.'

The pilot mumbled something under his breath and relapsed into a sullen silence. Richard Burdon turned away and waited till there was only Hartmann left. He helped him load and closed the hatch.

'Okay,' he shouted. 'We're through! Think of us tonight in the mess!'

'Yeah, I'll worry myself sick – in a pig's eye!'

With a roar the plane's engine came to life and the wind tore the breath out of Richard's mouth.

'Come on!' Hartmann bellowed above the noise; 'let's get away from here before the Vopos are on our necks!'

Richard gripped the other half of the handle and together they pulled the cart across the rough ground to where Krause stood. Quickly he filled the top with manure. By the time they had reached the road, the roar of the plane's engine had died away in the distance. Presently their pace slackened and they stopped for Hartmann to light a cigarette.

'That was an American in the aeroplane?'

Hartmann said.

'Yes.'

'I knew because he was scared.'

'How did you know, Hartmann, when you do not even speak English?'

'You don't need to know what the words mean to know when a man's scared. Besides, there are other ways. You can smell fear. I could smell that fat American's fear.'

'You don't like Americans, do you, Hartmann? Wall-Street capitalists and all that? Eh?'

Hartmann said nothing. They trudged on dourly.

'You were in the Party, weren't you, Hartmann?' Richard said after a pause.

'What Party?'

'You know what Party I mean.'

'Yes, I was; but what's it to you?'

'What are you doing in this, then? Why aren't you up there with the big boys, Pieck, Grotewohl, Ulrich – and the rest – an old comrade like you?'

'Don't call me that, Ami. It's a long story.'

'We've got plenty of time till we reach town. I've always got plenty of time for long stories. They're always the best, you know.'

Hartmann didn't answer.

'I was in the Party myself once, you know.'

'But you're an Ami.'

'Yes, but there were plenty of Amis as well as Tommis in the Party once. But why did you leave, old comrade? What was it with you? The pact or Finland. Perhaps not Finland – nobody'd heard of Finland. Was it Warsaw, then, or Berlin? It was all going to be different in the thirties, Hartmann, wasn't it? All different; and look where it ends up. Look where we are tonight!'

'Shut up, man!' Hartmann said thickly.

'Don't get angry, Comrade. Not that. I have a feeling that you've still got a little bit over for them. Don't you still believe a little in the truth? Just a bit of it, anyway?'

'Man, I hate them. And hate's a lot better than just belief, I've found out. It's a warm feeling and good, and keeps you going a lot longer than anything else...'

The old man, Krause, coming up behind, shouted a warning, but it came too late. He'd been keeping his eyes on the road – they hadn't. Now they came climbing out of the ditch; dark silhouettes in the gloom in the road some twenty or thirty metres in front of them.

'Vopos!' Hartmann bellowed at the top of his voice, and thrust his hand in his pocket.

'Halt!' a voice shouted, and Hartmann

fired from inside his pocket.

'Through the hedge, old man!' Richard shouted at Krause and started running, crouched low. As he ran, he fired, and he heard a groan and the clatter of a rifle on the cobbles. Hartmann stopped.

'Come on!' he shouted, grabbing Hartmann's arm. But Hartmann shook himself free, and fired again.

'I'm not leaving these,' he panted.

Somebody opened up with a sub-machine gun, and sparks and metal flew up from the road a yard in front of them. Richard burst through the hedge, the twigs tearing and ripping at his face and clothes.

'Hartmann!' he shouted, and the bullets burst into the hedge like heavy summer rain.

There was no reply, and in the light of the flare that went up he saw Hartmann frozen white, as if for eternity, kneeling behind the cart, his face sweating, it seemed, his lips drawn back in a kind of smile. Then again the leaves all round were whipped and threshed with lead, and he started back. He collided with the old man. Seizing his sleeve, they ran zig-zagged, crouched low, across the bumpy field towards the cover of the thick, dark pine-forest a hundred metres away.

CHAPTER SEVEN

They had taken Hartmann within ten minutes. He wounded two of them, but when his nine shots ran out, they came across and took him; it was no use running. They were only youngsters for the most part, eighteen- and nineteen-year-olds, and they were scared, so they didn't beat him up. Someone even gave him a cigarette, which was what he needed.

Within five minutes of being taken, however, he had begun to tremble badly. He wished he had been finished off straight away. It was nearly eight years since the last time, and he'd had eight years to think about it in the long nights when he couldn't sleep. He'd had eight years to develop nerves. Every time one of his escort lit a cigarette, he turned his eyes that way. But he didn't get another one. He wished he would. It would help.

At the barracks, in the cells behind the guard-room, Klein and Petersen took him over. He knew both of them well. With

Klein he was almost on 'thou' terms, and they'd got drunk together a few times after the 'Capitulation'. They were both small, fat men with receding hair-lines, who always looked as if they needed a shave. Both were professional police officials. Both had abnormally long arms with very thick wrists.

Klein was chewing a cigar when they brought him in. He waved to the guard to get out and nodded to Hartmann. Hartmann knew the nod: it meant strip. He began to take his clothes off, putting them neatly over the back of the chair. Klein looked at the ceiling, but Petersen watched him the whole time. Finally he was naked. For the first time in eight years he began again to whisper his little prayer that they wouldn't do that to him. He could stand a lot, but he knew he couldn't stand that. He thought Klein wouldn't, but he didn't know so much about Petersen. The latter was looking hard at the lower half of his body. He felt himself beginning to sweat. He knew they could do it. He had heard of it being done. He bit his bottom lip to stop it from trembling and said his little prayer over again.

'All right, then,' Petersen said quietly. 'Let's have a look at our exits and entrances, shall we?' He had heard those words often enough before.

They began to examine him. They were rough and crude, but that was nothing new. He bent down when they told him, and didn't shy when Petersen pulled on the rubber glove. It was the same as it always had been. He straightened up when they told him to, and then Petersen threw him his trousers. Hartmann tried a joke, as he pulled them on. 'Na ja, if it's like that, Miss, then we'll put our pants on again.'

Petersen smiled lazily and nodded to Klein. Hartmann bent his head to do up his flies, and Klein hit him in the face hard. He let go of his pants with the shock and pain of it and they sank absurdly to his knees. Klein hit him again and again – in the body, on the face. He hit him about two dozen times, then he went back to his chair and sat down. He was breathing fairly heavily, but was in no way flushed or angry. Hartmann sagged against the wall. He hadn't the strength to pull up his pants. He considered for a moment whether to drop and pretend he was out but rejected the idea. They wouldn't let him get away with it.

This was known as the 'erste Abreidbung' – the first rubbing-down. It had always been like this, ever since there had been a police force. Klein and Petersen had been doing it ever since they had joined the police. They did it without excitement and anger. It was just part of their duty, and they did it as conscientiously as they would warn someone for speeding or riding without a light.

Petersen got up and carefully laid his stump of cigar on the edge of the table. Hartmann stared at the slimy end he had had in his mouth, as if hypnotized. Then Petersen was in front of him and slapping him about the face – left, right, left, right, left, right. It went on for quite a long time, his head snapping from side to side. Petersen's blurred features always vanishing again just as his eyes were about to focus. He could hear Petersen begin to breath heavily, his breath coming through his throat noisily, as if he suffered from asthma. Then suddenly the slapping stopped, and he heard Petersen's voice in his ear. 'Man, they're going to soft-boil you. Watch it!' The next moment a bony knee caught him in the groin and the dark shutter fell in front of his eyes and his stomach flowed out of his body sickeningly. He went down on his face. 'Die erste Abreibung' was over.

He wasn't altogether out. But he was not going to move, not even open his eyes. He held every muscle of his body tight, not allowing himself to breathe too hard, trying to contain the thick, sickly pain which he could pin-point so exactly.

'To Mr Captain Wagner?' he heard Petersen say.

'Comrade Captain Wagner,' Klein corrected him. 'That's right.'

'I'm sorry. I always forget.'

'Es ist schon gut. It is already good. Let's take him across. I'm tired. The night shift takes it out of me these days...'

The two policemen bent down over him. Hartmann could hear them grunting short-windedly.

'His clothes,' Petersen said suddenly. 'The kitchen-woman might see him. I shouldn't like that.'

'No, I should not either.'

They pulled Hartmann's trousers on and hung his jacket over his shoulders, fastening it with the top button like a cloak.

They dumped him in front of Wagner and left after getting Wagner's signature 'for the body'. It was a joke, but Wagner didn't laugh. He looked at Hartmann's red, battered face for moment. Then he helped him into a chair and forced his usual smile, pushing his peaked cap to the back of his head with that practiced flick of his thumb and forefinger. He sat down facing Hartmann and put his boots on an open drawer.

'Na, altes Haus!' he said cheerily. 'Like old times again.' But the words didn't seem to come right, somehow.

Hartmann said nothing.

'You're getting old, Hartmann. A pig will never grow so old.' He had to take his eyes off the battered face. 'Here, let's have a little 'un?' He bent down and pulled out a bottle from his desk. He poured out two glasses. When Hartmann refused to reach over for his, Wagner got up and handed it to him.

'Pour that down behind your collar, old house,' he said. He was grateful when Hartmann picked up his glass.

He drained his own glass. 'Hals und Beinbruch! No broken bones, eh!'

Hartmann didn't look at him, but drank with his eyes fixed on the glasses. He drank slowly, in small sips, as if he wanted to make it last a long time. Wagner remembered the times in Sachsenhausen, and he opened his mouth to say something, but the words just wouldn't come. He swallowed hard and stuck his cigar back in his mouth. When at last he did speak, he chewed it from side to side wetly.

'Hartmann, I always say free from the liver. Straight out. So here it is. I don't suppose the big shots like it the way I do it. But anyway how are they going to know – unless you tell 'em, eh?' He winked at Hartmann and laughed. He was a little disappointed that Hartmann did not smile, but he went on in the same cheery manner as before: 'You've got to excuse Klein and Petersen. They're still living in the past. They think you've got to push a prisoner about before he'll tell you what you want to know. But that's not so. I know it's not so. They never got anything out of me that time, for all the pushing about. But, then, that's another story, isn't it, old house?'

'Get on with it,' Hartmann said wearily.

'Well, I think if you talk sensible to a prisoner – reasonable, like I'm doing to you, appeal to his senses, he'll respond. Don't you think that?'

'Man, don't tear out a leg!' Hartmann was beginning to lose his temper.

Wagner wasn't angry. He ignored the remark. 'So, old house, you're a sensible man. You know me. I know you. All right, then, to give the child a name. Where did the guns come from that they found in your cart?'

'What guns?'

'Komiker!' Wagner laughed heartily. 'What guns! That's funny!' He threw back his head and laughed, and Hartmann could see the mark the rope had left that time at Sachsenhausen. But that had been a long time ago. Wagner's eyes had filled with moisture from laughing and spittle had dribbled down his mouth. He wiped it away with the back of one of his big hands. 'Na, ja. Fun must be,' he said, gasping for breath. 'But now let's get down to it. Man,' he urged, 'you know me. With me you could steal horses. You can rely on me.'

Wagner spread out his hands. 'Look at my hands,' he said. He nodded at the knuckles, corrugated with rough work and spotted black just underneath the skin. 'See them knuckles. They're working-men's hands, like yours. Be sensible, man. Don't fight against your own kind.'

'Your own kind!' Hartmann exploded, his eyes sparkling. 'Turn your fat paws over and let me see the other side! No,' he said triumphantly, as Wagner hesitated. 'No, you won't do that, will you? Because they're as soft as yer big fat arse! You couldn't do a good day's hard work now if they were paying you a thousand marks an hour! No, they've made you soft here – living like God in France, with yer fancy women and yer big cars! All you are is a big fat fake living on yer past. You're not the Willi Wagner I knew once!' He paused for breath. 'Give me a drink,' he said quietly.

Wagner filled his glass without a word and handed it back to him. Hartmann drank it in a gulp.

Wagner opened his mouth, but for a moment no words came. 'Hartmann,' he said softly. 'It's not been easy. It's–'

'Hold your snout!' Hartmann shouted.

And then suddenly the tenseness went from Wagner's face again. He laughed, but there was no merriment in his eyes. 'A fat fake! Hartmann, you're the right one. You'll never learn, will you? Always straight-out.' He pressed the button on his desk and straightened his cap. Hartmann got to his feet without being told. They waited. A moment before the door opened to admit a uniformed policeman, Wagner asked softly. 'Will you? Please, Hartmann. Please.'

'Ach, klau' mir am Arsch!' Hartmann said angrily and turned away.

Wagner waited a long time before he sent for Todt. He sat there looking at his hands, and then he forced himself to press the bell.

'I'm giving you the man Hartmann, Comrade Lieutenant,' he said and watched for a reaction.

There was none. Todt waited politely.

'He's yours. You know what I ... we want.'

Todt straightened his pince-nez. 'Am I to deal with it the way I want, Comrade Captain?'

Wagner hesitated. 'Yes, I suppose so, Todt. Yes, the way you want. I'm taking the day off tomorrow.' He rubbed his hands down his face, and yawned. 'It's been a long night. I think I'll sleep it out tomorrow.'

He looked up at Todt's expressionless face. 'You won't–' he began, then he nodded to Todt that he was dismissed.

After Todt had gone he sat for a long time staring at his hands; it must have been nearly a full half-hour.

CHAPTER EIGHT

Hartmann lay on the plank bed and looked at the naked bulb in its cradle of barbed wire. The warder passed again and peered in at him through the Judas Hole. Hartmann pretended to sleep. Every ten minutes. He came every ten minutes, then.

Hartmann got off the bed and began to search the cell feverishly. Systematically he went over every object it contained. The plank bed, but it was held together with wooden joints and not nails. The lavatory, but there was no chain; it was flushed by a button. He ran his fingers round the dirt at the edge of the wall underneath the bed. Nothing, Null, comma, nothing. No glass. No metal. He stared down at his bed. At the worst he could tear the rough sacking of the mattress into strips and use that, but it wasn't a way he liked. He laughed a little bitterly to himself. A way he liked. That was funny.

He went to the water-tap in the corner and traced the course of the pipe down the wall till it disappeared into the floor. Sometimes they were held to the wall with metal clamps that you could sharpen on the stone. This one wasn't, though. So that was out. Time was passing. He must find something soon. He wouldn't get a second chance. He picked up a battered enamel water-mug from the floor, and turned it over. Then he had it. He clenched his fist round the handle and struck it against the stone of the cell wall. It made a lot of noise, but the mug was only dented. He struck it against the wall again and again. He heard feet coming down the corridor and he swung the mug again desperately. This time the enamel cracked: a long double crack half-way down the mug. He threw it on the bed quickly and turned his back to the wall. The keys rattled in the lock and the bolt was drawn noisily.

A heavily-built warder came in and looked at Hartmann sourly.

'Mensch, was hast du denn?' he asked.

'I am hungry,' Hartmann said calmly.

'Hungry! I'll give you hungry!' the policeman said. 'Don't make any theatre here!' He walked up to Hartmann and punched him in the face so that he staggered against the wall. Blood came out of Hartmann's nose. The policeman looked at him a moment, then went out. 'So'n Theater,' he said grumpily and locked the door behind him.

Hartmann tried to breathe in deeply, but he felt a sharp pain inside his nose and something moved. He started to breathe through his mouth. When the footsteps up the corridor had died away, Hartmann sat down on the bed and began to break the sliver of enamel from the mug.

It was difficult. The enamel stuck hard to the iron. One after another he broke the nails of his right hand. The work was exacting and he sweated. But it made him a little happy. He was beating them. That was the thing, he was beating them.

He broke off another bit of his thumb-nail and sucked the blood for a moment until it stopped, then went on with the work patiently.

An hour later he had freed two slivers of enamel from the mug: one half an inch long and the other about two inches and pointed towards the end. He breathed out and smiled to himself. The muscles of his hand hurt from the strain, but he hardly noticed them. He got up and rubbed the edge of the longer piece of enamel upon the stone window-sill. After some time rubbing, he spat on the enamel and rubbed it clean on the sleeve of his jacket. Satisfied, he drew it along the inside of his wrist, just above the hand. He scarcely felt it. After a moment when nothing happened, a thin line of blood broke through.

Almost happily he sat down on the edge of the plank bed. He had done it. He was safe. It would do. But where to hide it?

He looked round. The lavatory. He got up, grabbed a handful of thick newspaper and stuffed it down the bowl so that it was blocked. Then he wrapped the enamel in another piece and placed it on top. He undid his flies and urinated the best he could, though it hurt, over the paper. He finished and looked down into the bowl. He was satisfied. The Vopos wouldn't be too eager to put their hands in there. He buttoned up his flies and went over to his bed and lay down.

He was safe now. He could be brave when they came to fetch him. He wouldn't have to sing like a little yellow canary. The thought of the two slivers of enamel warmed him through and through, and after a time he fell into a sleep which was almost dreamless.

2

No light entered the boarded window of his

cell, but he judged that it was already day when they came for him. He felt sick and the light hurt his eyes and his legs didn't want to function correctly. They stood him in the centre of a low-roofed – it was only a foot above his head – stone-floored room.

'On the X,' the policeman who had brought him snapped.

Stupidly he looked round till he found the X painted in white on the floor. He stepped on to it.

'Stay there,' the policeman said and left. He was alone in the room.

Suddenly the light went out. He waited and nothing happened. A feeling of panic swept over him that was hard to fight. In the darkness he could hear them breathing. They were all round the walls, breathing and waiting. The black, tight panic made him almost gasp for air. He wanted to scream. With difficulty he controlled himself. He swallowed hard and breathed in shallowly through his mouth.

'Come on, then,' he said, hard and controlled. 'Out with the dung!'

The darkness came to life. A click and a blaze of lights hit him hotly from four sides. He looked upwards and the bulbs danced before his eyes. He looked down and the light pierced his eyelids redly. For a moment he was attacked by the fear that they were going to burn him. And then he controlled himself once more.

'I am going to ask you three questions,' a voice said suddenly. 'To which you are going to give me three simple answers. Remember that. Three simple questions and three simple answers.'

Hartmann tried to penetrate the wall of light, but failed. His eyes watered badly and he wiped them with the heel of his hand.

'These are the questions,' the voice said. 'Are you ready? One. Where did you get the weapons from?' There was a slight pause. 'Two. For what purpose are they intended? Three. Who are your accomplices? These are the questions. Please answer them now. In order.'

The lights seemed to be burning the air. Hartmann's face was bathed in sweat. He was sure that he could hear the lights burning up the air. He couldn't stand the silence any longer. Let 'em start if they wanted.

'I have nothing to say,' he said.

There was a pause.

'Don't be misled by loyalty to people or causes,' the voice said. 'Even if we fail to get the answers from you – and I assure you that we won't – we shall invent your own answers. They will run as follows. The weapons were landed by American saboteurs. They are intended for reactionary revolutionary purposes. And your accomplices. Well, anyone will do for those. We might take the first ten people in the Marx-Engelstrasse. You see, your silence will serve no purpose. Your death in pain will be of no value.'

'I have nothing to say,' Hartmann said, and tried again to penetrate the wall of light. The battery of bulbs danced before his eyes dizzily and made him sway to one side.

'On that X!' somebody shouted gruffly.

Beyond the light he heard whispering. For some reason it sounded funny to him. Like two old spinsters gossiping. Then silence. A moment later a click and the lights went out. Hartmann swayed and would have fallen had it not been for the hands that took him on both sides. They walked him away from the X, their boots ringing out on the stone flags of the floor. They walked along to where he felt instinctively that there should be a wall. He shrank back a little, expecting to walk into it, but they pulled him on. There was no wall. They were moving down a slope. Hartmann felt cold air on his face. He wished to God that they would put the lights on again, so that he could see where he was and what they were doing. They stopped and the hands let go and disappeared into the darkness again. There was silence.

'March four paces forward,' the same voice as before said from somewhere in the darkness.

Hartmann hesitated. 'Four, I said,' the voice commanded.

Hartmann wondered how they could see in the darkness, then started walking.

One, two, three.

He stopped suddenly. He had put his foot in water.

'Four,' the voice said harshly.

'It's water.'

'Four!'

He took another pace forward and the water was above his boots.

'You are now standing at four paces,' the voice said. 'The water comes up to your ankles. When I give the word, you'll move forward another four paces. Then the water will be up to your knees. At sixteen paces it is two metres deep – well over your head. Move forward eight paces.'

Hartmann hesitated.

'Well, are you going to speak?' the voice asked.

Hartmann moved forward the four paces. The water came up over his knees.

'There are now eight paces between you and drowning,' the voice said. 'Eight.'

Then there was silence.

Time went by and Hartmann stood there, his legs slowly being numbed by the ice-cold water. A few metres in front of him he sensed a wall. It was like being in a huge gutter. And they were going to smother him in its depths. He wanted to scream out for light. In the light it wouldn't be so bad.

'You are now at eight paces,' the voice said. 'I'm losing my patience rapidly. Are you going to speak?'

'No!' Hartmann shouted. 'No!'

'Then show him what I mean!' the voice screamed.

Heavy boots clattered over the stones and came running into the water. Hartmann turned round. Powerful hands reached out for him. He tried to fight them, but it was useless. A leg pressed against the back of his knee and he was pushed backwards and under. Hands grabbed his ankles. He came up spluttering and gasping for breath. The hands pulled his ankles upwards and he went under again, swallowing water in his struggle for air. He tried to control himself, but failed. He urinated in his trousers and did not even notice it. Between coming up and going under he told himself that they would stop before he drowned, but he didn't believe it himself. He went under and came up again. His chest threatened to burst. He lost control of his body. The roaring in his ears grew louder and louder. It was like a train roaring deeper and deeper into a black-red tunnel. He came up again, and this time he was screaming: 'I'll tell you! I'll tell you!' He screamed the words through the water that threatened to drown his lungs. For a moment he thought they were going to let him drown, and he struggled more violently than before, and then they were dragging him by the ankles through the shallow water; his chest heaving and sucking in the thin air in huge gulps.

They gave him time to recover, and he lay there and concentrated on breathing.

Then the voice was asking calmly as at first: 'Ready now? Ready now?' There was a hint of tiredness, of unnecessary effort in the two words.

'Please come closer,' Hartmann croaked thickly. 'I can't speak loud.'

'I'm here,' the voice said. 'Not a metre from you.'

Hartmann reached up a hand and felt through the darkness. He felt a face, spectacles, and then the face moved back startled, as if it had come in contact with something unclean.

'Please do not do that,' the voice said.

'Sorry,' Hartmann panted. He breathed in deeply, fixing his eyes on the spot in the darkness from where the voice had come.

'Answer,' the voice said.

Hartmann took one last deep breath. 'Here's your answer!' he shouted and struck out at the darkness.

His fist struck something solid, slid a little and then smashed into something soft. There was a tinkle of glass on the floor and Hartmann's fist was suddenly warm and wet. An unnatural high scream of pain and rage echoed against the stone walls.

'Er hat mich geblendet! He's blinded me, the swine!'

The lights went on suddenly and Hartmann had a glimpse of a Vopo officer, with a pale face and blood covering the bridge of his nose, shattered spectacles hanging askew. Then they were on him. 'I've done it,' he told himself joyfully, as the first blow sent his head flying back hard against the wall behind him. 'I've done it.' The officer was still screaming when the light went out.

3

He came to on his bunk. He tried to raise his head, but he couldn't. He tried again after a time and something gave and wetted his face. He opened his eyes and focused them on the mattress. It was soaked with blood where he had bled into it. He looked at it for a long time and then he turned his head slightly to the light. It felt as if two iron prongs were being forced upwards into the back of his head towards his eyes. He let his head fall again, swamped in the mist that surrounded it.

As he lay there he tried to feel his body. He couldn't. Everywhere it was fiercely hot and yet at the same time numb. He lay there quite a long time then and felt sorry for himself. If he had had the energy he would have cried in the great pity that he had for himself.

Then after a while he moved his head again. The prongs gave way to a vice that slowly tightened the grip on his left eyeball. He ignored the pain and slowly focused his eyes on the lavatory. It seemed a long way off and wouldn't keep quite still. After what could have been hours or minutes he dropped himself over the side of the bunk and crawled over to the bucket. The effort exhausted him and he was forced to lie there a while and recover his strength before he could sit up. He did so with difficulty, as the ribs on his left side no longer seemed to give him any support. After much effort and pain, he dropped his hand into the bowl and brought up the dripping wet package of newspaper with the enamel.

He unwrapped the paper and fingered the two slivers of enamel lovingly, turning them over in his battered fingers. They were almost beautiful. Clutching them tightly to him, he crawled back to his bed. He didn't take very long to get in, but it was fully five minutes before he got his breath again.

He lay there and held his arm up a little so that he could see the wrist. Then, holding the large sliver in his right hand, he put it on to the left wrist where the old scar was. He felt a slight prick of pain. A white dot appeared in the blue of the scar and disappeared quickly again.

He did it again, pressing a little harder this time. There was a small hole in the blue. Fascinated he watched the white pit in the blue fill red and then blue again. He watched until there was no trace of the white left. He examined his wrist carefully to see this. And then, almost savagely, as if he were doing it to another person, he dug the sliver deep in his wrist, and drew it along the length of the old scar. He changed hands and did it to his right wrist. The old scars opened easily and without much pain. His right wrist did not seem deep enough, but he couldn't bring himself to force the sliver into the wound. He laid the enamel down carefully and pulled the one blanket over him, allowing enough light to see his wrists.

The blood flowed slowly but steadily. He turned his wrists upwards, wounds towards him, so that he could see them better. He supposed that the blood would flow more quickly if he hung his hands downwards, but it gave him pleasure to watch the bleeding and he kept them upwards. It was like when he was a child and had read thrillers under the blankets when he should have been asleep.

But after a time he felt tired and he relaxed, closing his eyes. He relaxed completely. The blood flowed smoothly and warmed his whole body. It was like the Sunday mornings as a youth when he could stay longer in bed and he had let his mind run warmly from one girl to another. It was very pleasant. A golden glow seemed to emanate from somewhere round his navel and heat his whole body.

For the first time since he could remember, he felt happy. All the tenseness that had been his adult years vanished. He didn't hate anyone, and the driving force was drawn slowly and surely from his body. After a time he seemed to swell and rise like a balloon from the bed. Then he was outside himself, looking down at himself on the bed from a great height. This, he thought, was funny. It made him laugh, though he knew he should not laugh. A cradle-song from his youth came to him. He repeated it to himself.

'Sleep, little child, sleep.
Thy father watches the sheep.
Thy mother is in Pommerland.
Pommerland is burnt down.
Sleep, little child, sleep.'

He tried to sing it, but couldn't. He forced himself to try to sing it. Still he couldn't. A moment of panic. Of course he could stop it if he wanted. He tried to open his eyes. He couldn't. He gritted his teeth together and tried again. He couldn't. He swore at himself. Still he couldn't.

Then the lazy feeling came over him again. He seemed to sink deeper and deeper into the bed. He would wake up in a minute and then everything would be all right again. In exactly one minute ... one minute ... one... The very next minute, he promised himself ... one ... one... And then he was dead.

CHAPTER NINE

In the late evening they found Hartmann. The blood had almost trickled to the door. He was already cold. The word spread round the prison block. It was tapped on the central heating pipes from cell to cell. It passed into the yard as a whisper from the side of a mouth, and it went through the gates with the trustee who emptied the garbage cans. It wandered home drunkenly with one of the Vopos who had taken part in the water treatment. In the late evening they had found Hartmann.

The old man brought the news home with him from the lock. He came home from work in his damp, muddy overalls and sat down heavily on the wooden bench in the kitchen, without greeting any of them. His wife pushed a cup of coffee before him and looked at him from beneath lowered lids. But he let the coffee grow cold.

They sat and watched him and waited. Today, Richard Burdon thought, he really looks an old man, with his grey-stubbled, beaten face. Nobody said anything, and the old man himself was the first to break the silence.

'Hannes is dead. Hartmann's dead. He did away with himself last night. Cut his wrists. Bled to death before they found him.'

'He's bought it.' Unconsciously Richard expressed the thought in this way to himself. Next moment he hated himself. 'He's bought it.' It was one of those silly Anglicisms they had all used in those days. It had meant nothing, though they told themselves in their more vocal moments that it meant a lot more. But it meant nothing. They didn't know what emotion meant.

'What the hell's the matter with you?' the little voice inside him snapped. 'What the hell are you fussing about? Hartmann's out of the way now, isn't he?'

He forced himself to think logically. Now that Hartmann was out of the way he could get what he wanted. He could have the factory blown and he could take off with the girl. It would be easy. None of them had the strength of character that Hartmann had had. The old man hadn't nor Von Kornfeld.

The girl inclined her head towards the old man, and then at the door. Richard stared at the old man. He was gazing uncomprehendingly at the cold cup of coffee, his eyes full of tears. His wife was peeling potatoes on the chair, potato basket between her feet, but it was obvious that her mind wasn't on her work and she failed to peel them in her usual economic manner. Richard Burdon understood at last and rose to his feet. He followed the girl out without either of them saying a word. In silence they wandered across the meadow and then into the wood.

'I would have probably been forced to kill him, anyway.' Richard said suddenly. 'Didst thou know that?'

'Hartmann?' she said, surprised.

'Yes, Hartmann,' he said harshly.

'But why?' She tried to make him stop and look at her, but he dragged her on with him roughly.

'He stood in my way. He wanted to fight in the factory. I didn't; I wanted to blow it and then go.'

She didn't say anything.

'Blow it and then go.' He emphasized the words again brutally.

Still she didn't say anything. He was forced to ask his own question.

'Why? Because I don't believe in this revolt of theirs. It can't succeed. Everything is against them. And they'll get no support from the other side. That's just another lie. I've told nothing but lies since I've been here. All I've believed in was thirty thousand dollars and a little house that may not even exist any more.' He stopped and held her close to him. 'Dost thou know how much thirty thousand dollars is?'

She shook her head numbly.

'It's half a million East Marks! Half a million! It's freedom!' He lowered his voice. 'Say something, Stine.'

'What shall I say? Thou art suddenly quite different. I do not know thee so.' She shook herself free and walked on. After a moment he followed her.

'Stine,' he said low and urgent, 'listen to me. This is what I believe. This thou must hear. I believe in the individual. Thou understands this word? It is difficult in German.'

'Yes, I understand,' she said tonelessly.

'Good. I believe in myself as an individual. A long time ago I have come to the belief that there is only one tragedy in this life. That is death. The so-called tragedies of nations are not important in comparison with this. Death is all important. And death is with one from the start. One is born and one dies. One is in love and one dies. One copulates and one dies. The last is a polite word, but it is the only one I know for it in German.'

'Is it when we are together?' she asked softly.

'Yes.' Her question put him off. 'Always, Stine … there is only once – the first time, and after that death and never again. That is the only tragedy that there is. Since I have discovered this, many things have become of little importance to me. And those that are important have become sad. Dost thou understand?'

'Yes, I think I do,' she said slowly. 'But I have never thought like this!'

'It is because thou art young and not experienced. The feeling comes with age, though often those who have the age refuse to accept it.' He paused for breath. 'It is not a good feeling, but in many ways it is sad and noble.'

They walked on in silence for a time.

'But why dost thou tell me this?' she asked, and she took his hand as they began to climb the hill.

The smallness and warmth of her hand made him feel good.

'Because I wanted thee to understand me. This revolt has no chance. And if it did have it would still be of no importance. One thing alone is important – us. That is all.'

'And my father and the others, what of them?' she asked simply.

Across the valley came the sound of the siren from the factory. Both of them turned for a moment and stared at the factory's metallic towers glinting dully in the thin, cold sunlight that escaped the black clouds.

'I don't know – about them,' Richard said lamely. 'I had not thought about them.'

The siren stopped and they walked on in silence until they reached the spot where they had been the time before. They sat down automatically. They didn't talk for a long time.

Inside, the voice tried to rouse him to anger. What did he care about the old man and the rest? What did it matter if Hartmann had died? Weren't they and only they important? But the voice was failing. Slowly and heavily the rhythm pounded on and on. They couldn't. They couldn't run. They couldn't run now... They couldn't ... couldn't ... couldn't.

Her hand took his again and after a moment pressed it hard.

'Richard, is it so bad?' she asked.

He forced a smile, and shook his head. 'No, not really, I suppose. Just a "moralischen". I'll get over it.'

'Thou must, Richard,' she said softly.

'Yes, I know.'

She was suddenly very confident. 'It will go good, Richard. It will go good. I know it will.'

'Yes, naturally,' he said, infected a little by her mood.

'I think it will go good,' she said, 'because there are plenty of people like my father and the others all over the Zone who feel as he does. When it starts they will all come for sure. I have great faith in this. Listen, once when I was younger I went to church. I think it was Confirmation or something. When we leave school we are confirmed, though of course my father would never allow us to believe in that sort of thing. The Social Democratic Party is against it. Well, I went to this church, and I remember the man saying that everything was decided in advance. Things would go bad and then they would go good. This I remembered. Things would go bad and then they would go good. And I believe it. Things have gone bad so far. Now I think they must go good for us. They must, Richard. They must.' She gripped his wrist and contorted her face, as if trying to force them to go well by sheer strength.

'And I believe it too, Stine,' he said, capturing her enthusiasm again for a moment. 'I believe it.' And when he said the words, he believed them – or at least for a little while.

'In two days, then,' he said.

'In two days,' she echoed his words. 'And then we will go and I shall drive thy Ford.'

The clouds moved and a black shadow swept up the valley, over house and field and settled on the metallic towers of the factory.

CHAPTER TEN

It was early in the morning. The old man and his wife walked slowly across the yard to the shed where their son was hidden. The old man carried the coffee-pot and his wife the boy's food. They opened the door of the shed and went in. The boy was not on the bed they had made for him in the corner behind the bales of hay. He was sitting on the barrow and forcing his legs into his big top-boots the best he could with one arm.

The old man put down the coffee-pot quickly and went over to him.

'Be careful son,' he said anxiously. 'Thou must not open the wound again.'

The boy ignored him and went on grimly, beads of sweat standing out on his forehead, while his father looked on puzzled, a deep frown furrowing his brow.

Ignoring both of them, his wife poured out the coffee through the sieve, the dark brown liquid preceded by a wet lump of coffee-grains which fell heavily into the sieve.

'Why dost thou put on thy boots?' the old

man asked. 'If thou must walk, why not wear these?' He nodded down at his own heelless wooden slippers.

With a grunt the boy succeeded in getting his feet into the second of the boots. He stood up and stamped his feet on the dirt floor.

'I'm going back,' he said at last. 'I have made a mistake and I'm going back. I should never have gone over the hill in the first place. They aren't all like Schmidtkin.'

'But thou wilt be punished, man!' the old man said excitedly. 'Thou wilt certainly have to sit for some time.'

The boy shrugged his shoulders and accepted the cup that his mother handed him.

'So I will sit. A month, two months. What is that? I'm young. I have a lot of time.'

'Would that be all the punishment? One, two months?' his mother asked, speaking for the first time.

He nodded and took another drink of his coffee.

'So.' She looked at the old man. He read the look in her eyes.

'But that doesn't matter,' he said angrily, looking from one to the other. 'Dieter, it is a bad thing to go back to them. They kill and they make bad, and make it so that one may not speak the truth any more – and' – he hesitated – 'the young have no respect for the old.'

'Respect!' The boy lowered his cup. 'Dost thou think that I have respect for thee? For thy tumble-down house, for thy stinking closet, for thee and thy pamphlets? What respect can I have for thee? Didst thou have respect for thyself when the Fascists came? Tell me that. Please tell me that, if thou wilt.'

The old man said nothing.

'No, Father, I have respect only for the people who respect.'

'I respect thee,' the old man said quickly.

'I know, Father, but not like that. I mean the people who say that we don't have to wait till we're a hundred years old before we can open our mouths or because we haven't got the right accent. We young ones are im-portant now. And I'm just as good as the rich man's son – and better. Didst thou know that the burgomaster of Leipzig was only twenty-one when they made him Burgo-master? Didst thou know that today one can be made a judge at twenty-four? What did thy S.P.D. have to offer youth? A monthly meeting and sports club!' He finished his coffee with a gulp and set down the cup noisily on the saucer.

'But they're bad,' the old man persisted. 'They're very bad.'

The boy ignored him and began to slide his good arm into the sleeve of his tattered tunic. He didn't quite manage it, and his mother went over and helped him. He thanked her and looked again at his father.

'It's no use, Pappa,' he said softly. 'We'll never understand each other now.' He smiled. 'We never have, have we, really? Ever since I have been old enough to think for myself we've been in each other's hair.' He reached out his good hand, as if to touch his father, and then slowly drew it back again, when the old man ignored the hand.

The old woman began to button up his jacket for him while he looked down at the ground, avoiding his father's eye. The old man watched his wife's split thumb awkwardly turning the buttons. He remembered the time she had split it, chopping wood in the shed one dark winter's morning. He realized suddenly she was with the boy. For a moment anger mounted up within him and he wanted to go over and strike her to the ground like he might have done when he was young. And then his mind wandered off stupidly and he thought of the time when he

151

first met her. Then she would have been for him and for him only, he told himself. Hedwig – he tried to remember her maiden name and couldn't. Hedwig. He had never called her anything but that at first. And now it was just 'Mother'. There had been a lot of names since then, but now it was just 'Mother.'

'Mother,' he said, as if trying the word out for the first time. 'Mother, stop it. If he wants to go, let him get himself ready.'

The old woman took no notice, but went on with her work.

The old man was no longer angry with her. He was more sad than anything, and then puzzled. His eyes travelled down to the back of her legs, violet striped in their heavy grey woollen socks, and up again to the black dress she had always worn since she had come into the forties. With this woman, he thought, he had spent thirty years of his life. Together they had done good, bad, bestial, beautiful things. They had worked together in the cornfields of their youth, when the heat-haze rippled over the still corn and the heat struck you almost a physical blow on the back of the neck. They had strained the winter's nights away in the big, sweating, protesting bed. They had brought forth children, and he had stood and watched her grip the brass rail of the bed with her thick, scarred hands and her lips had bared back from her black teeth and she had looked at him like an animal, but no sound had come from her lips.

All this they had done together, and yet suddenly she was a stranger to him, and he couldn't even remember the name she had brought with her.

'Hedwig,' he said softly, trying the sound of the new name on his tongue. 'Hedwig.'

But the old woman did not turn round, and if she had heard him she showed no sign of having done so.

The boy was ready. He put his good hand on his mother's head for a moment. 'I'm going now, Mamma,' he said, attempting a smile.

'It will be only a month or two – thou art certain?' she asked.

He nodded encouragingly. 'Of course, little mother. Of course. Don't worry.'

'Then go. Go with God.'

'There is no God, Mamma.'

'Naturally. I have not forgotten. It is just a saying that one uses.'

He stretched out his hand to his father. 'Goodbye, Father.'

The old man ignored the outstretched hand. 'Thou dost not go,' he said firmly. 'I shall not let thee go. Thou art too young to understand.'

'Machst gut, Pappa,' the boy said and then, lowering his eyes, pushed his way past.

The old man reached out and caught the boy's bad arm. He went white with pain and groaned. And then, with a swing of his other hand, he pushed his father backwards so that he overbalanced and fell over the remains of the winter store of potatoes.

The old man was winded, and it was a moment before he could get up. Gasping, and a little red in the face, he staggered to his feet and stood there undecided.

'It is for the best, Ewald,' his wife said, her hard face softening. 'The young must always have their will. One can't stop them.'

The old man ignored her. Then he went out and slammed the shed door behind him. He walked to the house and stood there, watching the boy moving quickly up to the road. Then he turned and went into the house and through into the kitchen.

In the kitchen Richard was listening to the radio. The news from the studio of the German Democratic Republic had just finished – a list of quotas promised by sugarbeet factories, threats by Ulbricht and news from the minor countries of Eastern Europe of which the ordinary German listener had probably never heard a few years before.

The old man came in, and Richard saw at once that something was the matter, but he did not say anything: he waited till the old man was ready.

The room was full of flies. A neighbour had asked permission to graze a horse in the meadow, and it had attracted them. The old man stood there and swatted the flies stupidly for quite a long time before he spoke.

'My son ... he's gone,' he said slowly.

'Gone where?'

'Back to his barracks.'

Richard sat up at once. He reached up and switched off the radio. 'Back to the barracks, you say! Man!'

'Yes. And if he starts talking about you, Mr American. You see.'

He concluded without saying what would happen. But Richard saw well enough without being told. He saw, and yet he held back from suggesting what he knew must be done. The old man looked at him hopefully, expecting an easy solution. But there was no easy solution.

The minutes passed and no one spoke.

'We'll have to stop him,' the old man said suddenly. 'Won't we?' The sentence trailed off.

Richard Burdon nodded his head.

The old man drew himself erect, as if he were throwing a weight from his shoulders. 'Will you come with me, American?' he asked.

'Where?'

'To the telephone.'

'The telephone?'

'I know how to stop him.'

They walked down the road in silence. Richard did not ask the old man what he intended to do. They came to the yellow-painted telephone-box, with the eagle and post-horn painted on the side. The old man hesitated. 'Will you help me, please? I have never telephoned.'

'Yes, I'll help you.'

They crushed into the box and the door swung to behind them.

'Whom shall I call for you?' Richard asked the old man.

The old man looked straight ahead at the wall covered in pornographic drawings and the scribble of names and dates. 'The police.'

Richard picked up the elegant old-fashioned instrument and pressed in the twenty pfennigs. He got the police and handed the phone to the old man. The old man accepted it, holding the thin cross-piece as if it were very delicate. It was very hot in the box and the sweat stood out on his brow and clung to the thick bushy hair of his eyebrows.

Carefully he put the phone to his mouth, but when he opened it to speak no words came. He looked across appealingly at Richard. From the other end came the thin crackle of sound. Richard didn't say anything. Then the old man spoke: 'I want to report a deserter from the flag. Yes. Dieter Krause. Stationed at Salzwedel. Yes, I said Salzwedel with the Barracked People's Police there. Yes, yes. He will cross the border black tonight, he told me. He should be there now! Oh,' and here the old man's voice grew warm for a moment, 'tall and thin. Fine light hair. Wound in one arm. Yes, that's right.

'My name? It doesn't matter!' He took the phone away from his mouth and stood staring at it numbly. His old black-veined hand, covered with the freckles that come with age, trembled slightly. From the other end came the crackle of inquiring, puzzled sound.

Gently Richard released his hand from the phone and laid it back in its cradle. The old man allowed him to do it without protest.

They went out into the fresh air; its coolness after the heat of the box made them shiver a little.

'It will be all right,' he said persuasively. 'They don't shoot deserters in peace time.'

'And if they send him away? They sometimes send them away,' the old man said brokenly.

'Soon our day will come, and he will be freed before they have time to do that. Soon.'

The old man pinched the loose flesh of his nose between his thick thumb and forefinger. 'Soon,' he said. 'Soon.'

2

Late that afternoon they left him alone with Lieutenant Todt. He was wounded and, besides, the lieutenant had his pistol, so it was safe. They dumped him on the chair in front of the lieutenant's desk, and when they let go, his head slumped forward on to the edge of the desk.

Lieutenant Todt looked at the tousled blond hair for a long time. Now that the bloodied, battered face was no longer to be seen, it was almost beautiful. He was only a boy and there was something fresh and innocent about him. It was a pity about the face, of course.

Slowly the boy came to himself. 'It's true,' he moaned, 'It's true.'

Lieutenant Todt pulled off one of his white gloves and laid it on the desk, carefully picking a spot where no dust would get on it. Gently, and trembling a little in spite of himself, he reached out his hand and touched the boy's hair. It was soft and fine and warm like a girl's, like a beautiful innocent young girl's. He experienced an empty hot excitement inside him; it was as if his insides had left him and he was no longer capable of controlling the movement of his body. His hand trembled so that he could no longer stop it.

'Lift up thy head,' he said softly, having difficulty with his breathing.

Slowly the boy lifted his face and then his mouth filled and opened. It was too late. The lieutenant drew his hand back, but it was too late. The boy coughed thickly and the blood and bile flowed over the lieutenant's soft white hand.

'Du, Drecksau!' the lieutenant almost

screamed, and with his booted foot he sent the boy's chair from under him so that the boy went backwards, striking his head against the stone wall.

The boy lay there, his mouth open unpleasantly. 'True,' he breathed. 'True...'

'I'll give you true, you swine!' Lieutenant Todt shouted, and he pressed the bell on his desk before he even mopped up the mess on his hand. The boy started to whimper before they were in the door...

CHAPTER ELEVEN

They started coming just after it grew dark. They were freshly shaven, with red, clean faces, and here and there Richard noticed a man with a trace of shaving-soap behind his ear or where the hair met the skin. Most of them had clean shirts on, too, and the pockets of several of them bulged with packets of sandwiches. They arrived and stood around in the sandy yard chatting and smoking quietly, going to relieve themselves behind the trees rather often.

Richard moved among them, stopping here and there to exchange a few words, and he was embarrassed in the dark when they took their hands out of their pockets and spoke high German for his benefit. He listened to their plodding, awkward high German, lacking the ease of their daily dialect, and told himself over and over again what a rotten fake he was. There was no thirty thousand dollars in it for them, nothing much except perhaps a bullet. He couldn't stand their decency, and he went off by himself to the edge of the meadow until they started going inside the house.

There was schnaps and beer as before, but the men were reluctant to drink much.

'Have another one, man,' he heard someone say, as he pushed his way into the crowded room. 'Thou canst not stand on one leg alone.'

'No. It's enough, I think. I want to keep a clear head,' someone else answered.

The sound of the words and the simplicity of their answer hurt. Everything he heard and saw hurt. Why was it going to be them? What the hell had they ever done, for this to happen to them? They made him think of his father for the first time in years. He would have felt at home among these men even if he had not understood their words. Richard remembered him in his shirt sleeves at the kitchen table under the bad light, reading the evening paper, spelling out the words to himself. As he read he had followed the words with a thick, nicotined forefinger; flattened and splayed by years of hard work. About his father in the evening reading the paper in the kitchen there was something complete and satisfied. Everything was clear and straightforward, with no loose ends. His own life had not been like that. There had been plenty of loose ends. There had been more high spots about his than his father could ever have imagined, but there would never be the same satisfaction and completeness.

Someone gave him a drink, and he swallowed it at a gulp. It made him cough, but he accepted another. It was no use worrying now. It was too late. He couldn't stop it, even if he wanted to.

The old man pushed his way through the crowded room to his place near the stove. His cheeks seemed to have gone thinner since the morning, and there was a purpose about his face that Richard had never noticed before. He rapped the iron top of the stove for attention and started speaking almost at once.

'You've all heard about Hannes, I think. I don't know what to say. I only know it won't be forgotten. Not by me, at least. I remember him as a lad running about in his bare feet. And I was already an apprentice then. It doesn't seem right somehow that he should go before me.' The old man frowned. 'We'll remember him,' he said quickly. 'Hannes is gone, so we need someone to take charge.' He looked over at Von Kornfeld and Richard. 'I'll do it if you think it is all right? I know what Hannes intended to do.'

'Yes, Ewald, it's all right with us,' someone said.

'And me.'

'And me.'

'And me,' the others mumbled their approval.

'Good. Then that's settled. I have thought today who should do what. And I have decided like this. There are thirty-two of us. There would be more if we had the weapons, but we haven't. I divided us into groups like this. Four of you with the American.' The old man nodded over at Richard. 'Ten I shall take with me, and the rest will go with Von Kornfeld.' He stopped and let the words sink in. Richard looked at the old man, surprised at this change in him. He seemed a different man from the peasant that Richard had first met a few days before.

'These of you will go with the American,' the old man went on, and read the names of the four men. 'These with Von Kornfeld.' Again a list of names. 'And the rest then with me. Clear?'

'Clear.'

'Good. I shall do the forced labourers, Von Kornfeld the factory and the American will do the truck bringing the technicians, as he knows about the explosives. We've talked about it.' He stopped and let Richard explain.

'We shall mine the road from Melen about one kilometre from here. The four who will go with me will cover the road and see that no one escapes from the truck. That bit is important.'

Richard said the words without emotion, as he had said similar words often enough before, and then he stopped suddenly, seeing the meaning of the words reflected on his listeners' faces. There he saw the burning truck splayed stupidly across the road, the stink of the burnt rubber, the charred carcases, the noise, the sweat, the smell of – and he faltered for a moment. 'It should be … easy,' his voice died away.

The men looked at him curiously.

'Von Kornfeld will do the gate as Hannes planned it,' the old man took up the conversation again. 'By six-thirty we should be in the factory. And then' – he bent forward slightly and looked at them hard, his eyes moving round the room from face to face – 'we'll show them what we're made of.'

The men were embarrassed, ashamed of any emotion, and then they were relaxed again. Out came the cigars and the little amber-coloured pipes and the light, cheap cigarette-tobacco. Here and there a man pushed his way to the door.

'The rifles are in the shed,' the old man said above the rising murmur of chatter. ''08's they are. You'll all know how to use them.'

Here and there a man laughed.

'Ay, I'd like to have a Taler for every time I've used that banger,' someone said.

'One hundred rounds each for a start,' the old man said. 'The rest of the ammunition we'll bring up in the truck.'

Richard moved over to Von Kornfeld and waited patiently while the others filed out. He gave him good-evening.

'Evening,' Von Kornfeld said. 'How goes it?'

'It goes, thank you,' Richard said.

Von Kornfeld laughed.

'And you?'

'It goes so la-la.'

Richard laughed. 'It will be difficult at the gate, I have no doubt.'

'Perhaps. But with luck we will catch them off guard. It is a good time, six. Everyone will still be taken by sleep.'

'Yes, that is true. We will hope, in any case.'

'Yes, we will hope.'

166

They were both silent for a while, and watched the men leave, and then Richard said, 'Well, I must go and get my weapon ready. Till later.'

'Till later.'

2

They sat in the badly-lit kitchen, talking very little, the two men bent over their weapons. For himself Richard had selected a machine-pistol. It was good and accurate. Far too good for fighting. He knew that once dropped in the mud it was useless. But still it was very accurate at a fairly long range for a machine-pistol, and it made one confident to have such fire-power at one's disposal. He slipped out the long, thin magazine and began to force out its bullets with the point of his knife. The spring functioned well and evenly. He would have no stoppages, he felt. He emptied the magazine and started to smooth the metal of the spring with oil. Finishing this, he began filling the magazine again.

'It is good of the Americans to supply us with German weapons,' the old man said. He was sitting next to Richard bent over the trigger-guard of his rifle, spectacles balanced on the end of his nose. 'It makes it easier when they are familiar to one.'

'Yes,' Richard said laconically, and carried on with his work without looking up. The innocence of these people was embarrassing, he told himself. Good of the Americans to give them German weapons! They weren't going to be compromised as easily as that.

'Gib mir mal das Oel, Mamma,' the old man said without looking up. 'Give me the oil, Mamma.'

But his wife, sitting next to the oven in the corner, did not move.

The old man looked up at her, straining his eyes through the steel-rimmed spectacles. 'Mamma, das Oel,' he said. 'Didst thou not hear?'

The old woman did not say anything.

'Du hast wehl grosse Bohnen gegessen – thou hast eaten big beans, eh? that thou dost not hear,' he said.

'I heard thee well,' the old woman said calmly.

'Then why didst thou not answer?'

'Because I do not agree with thee and what thou art doing tonight.'

'It is no longer important that thou dost not agree,' the old man said quietly, his head

168

suddenly bent over the trigger-guard.

'That is true. That is true now,' his wife said reflectively. 'It is possibly too late now.'

'Yes, too late now, old woman,' the old man echoed her words.

She got up wearily from her chair in the corner and handed him the oil. He accepted it without looking up. There was silence in the room again except for the heavy tick of the cheap alarm clock on the plate near the window-sill.

'Ewald,' the old woman said suddenly, 'dost thou remember how we used to kill the pigs in the old days? Those were good times, were they not?' There was an enthusiasm in her voice which seemed strange coming from that hard old face.

'I remember, Mamma,' Stine said when the old man did not reply. 'I remember even though it was still when I was a child. They were killed in November, yes?' But neither her father nor her mother paid any attention to her.

'Dost thou remember, Ewald?' the old woman persisted.

'Yes, I remember.'

'And dost thou remember how we would scrub the skin for the hair? And how we would stir the blood still warm for the sausage? And how I'd fry a choice piece for thee and the inspector?'

'And how they boiled the meat and I was sick from eating too much,' Stine said excitedly. But still neither of them took any notice of her.

'Remember the cognac,' the old woman went on, 'and how thou became drunk that time when the inspector told us that we had two hundred pounds of meat? Das war aber ein Schwine! Dost thou remember that?'

The old man put down his weapon violently, his face red and angry. And then, after a moment, he took it up again and continued his cleaning. 'I remember, old woman,' he said calmly; 'but it is too late now.'

'But these were good times,' the old woman pleaded. 'Good times. And we were happy. I am sure that we were happy.'

'It is too late,' the old man said wearily. This time he looked up at her and shook his head from side to side sadly. 'Too late.'

'Too late?' the woman asked stupidly.

'Yes.'

For a moment the woman looked at him, and then slowly she got up from her chair.

'I shall go to bed now.' She picked up the battered old alarm clock from its plate and began to wind it up laboriously.

'It is set for the morning,' she said, and then realized what she was saying. She put it down again on its plate.

'It is the first time since we were married that I have never taken an alarm clock with me when I went to bed,' she said to no one in particular, almost as if she were speaking to herself.

She pulled her apron off over her head and hung it on the hook behind the door. She nodded to them each in turn. Stine half got to her feet, but changed her mind and sat down again.

Standing at the door, she looked at her husband. 'Nacht, Ewald,' she said.

'Nacht, Mamma.'

He lowered his eyes quickly and she went out.

3

Above the jagged line of the forest they watched the dirty white of the false dawn. It was almost four o'clock. They stood in the long, wet grass of the meadow and watched it hand in hand. Behind them in the yard there was a brief murmur of conversation, punctuated by a man's dry early-morning cough.

'It is difficult to talk in the morning,' she said.

'Yes, I agree. The words won't come,' Richard answered and kept his eyes on the skyline. It would be light soon.

'Thou wilt stay here till it is finished,' he said. 'Then I will come for thee.'

'No, I wish to come with thee, Richard. Thou wilt say it is dangerous. But because of that I want to be with thee. If it happens to thee … then let it happen to me too. Life has no worth for me without thee.'

Gently Richard pressed his hand over her mouth and stopped her speaking.

'Let us not talk of dying,' he said. 'It is not a good subject for this time of the day.'

They were silent again. Richard yawned and shivered a little. In the yard there was the dry rattle of the starter as they got the truck ready. It coughed once, twice and then roared into life. The driver revved the engine loudly so that they were deafened for a moment. Desperately she put her hands round his neck and bent him down to her. 'Richard, Richard. No! No!'

He allowed her to hold him, then he gently released himself from her grasp. 'I don't want to, Stine,' he said softly.

He kissed her. 'Stay here,' he whispered.

'Stay here, and don't turn thy eyes away from the forest till I am gone.'

'Richard.'

He pressed her hand and then he was gone, walking quickly through the long grass to where the men were climbing into the truck. No need to think any more now. It was June the Seventeenth. No more need to think.

THE END

CHAPTER TWELVE

Richard lay in the damp early morning grass and watched the road. Half an hour before they had broken the badly tarred surface in two places and laid the explosives in two groups – one in case the first did not function. Then he had posted his riflemen in position at the four corners of the box, in whose centre the truck bringing the technicians would explode. No one must escape and get back with the news to the factory.

The first rays of the sun filtered into the pine-trees around him, poking long, dusty-light-fingers into the ground-mist that you could almost feel. This was the part of the day that he had always liked best. Whatever had happened to him, he could never experience this part of the day without the feeling of hope that everything would go well. It had always been like that, and it always would.

Richard lay fairly relaxed in the grass, not

175

particularly worried by its dampness on his thighs and stomach and watched the world come to life again. Steam began to ascend from the grass where the sun hit it, and in the meadow beyond the road he could see rabbits moving quickly, nervously, between clipped hillocks. A bird began to sing quite close. He wondered what it was. He turned to the fat man, who was with him as a runner.

'What manner of a bird is that?' he asked.

The fat man jumped. He was very nervous. Richard felt sorry for him.

The fat man listened for a moment, his head turned into the wind. 'Das ist n'Drossel. I think so, at least.'

N'Drossel. A thrush. As boys they had always called it a 'throstle' in their own dialect. Throstle – the word came back to him again after all the years. It had lain submerged in his memory thirty years, to come up one morning in a German forest. The fact seemed important to him somehow.

Suddenly the fat man tugged at his sleeve. Richard screwed round his head.

'Excuse me, Sir,' the fat man said. He sounded like someone asking the way in a big city. It seemed strange to hear that kind of tone in these circumstances. Richard bit

back the desire to laugh. The fat man pointed to his rifle. 'I keep pulling this thing
back to ... eject the spent cartridges, you
said?'

'Yes, that is right.' Richard took the rifle
from him and slipped back the bolt. The
dull yellow cartridge flew out. 'So it is done,'
he said and reloaded. 'It's easy.'

'I am not so sure,' the fat man said. 'And I
don't want to make a mess of it when the
truck comes. You see, Sir, I wasn't ever a
soldier. I was too young for the first one and
my heart was too bad for the Volkssturm in
Archer's war. So you see–'

'Ruhig!' Richard whispered quickly.
'Listen!' He turned his head to the wind and
listened, the fat man watching him anxiously, tiny drops of sweat forming between
his nose and his upper lip.

Richard felt sure he could hear the rumble
of explosions and the faint, sharp crackle of
small-arms fire. He tried to force his ear to
a higher pitch of acuteness. He was sure he
could hear firing. Quickly he glanced at his
watch. Six o'clock. It must be the old man.
Silently he wished him luck.

'What was it?' the fat man asked. 'Please.'

'Krause's group, I think. We'd better keep
our eyes on the road. They'll be coming

soon now.'

The fat man sighted his rifle on the road, blinking nervously, like a raw recruit the day he fires on the range for the first time. Richard laid his hand on the plunger and stared at the road. His hands were beginning to sweat slightly. Let them come now, he prayed. Now.

The rabbits had moved from the meadow and were playing on the road. He told himself he was quite calm, and in the same moment noticed that he was breathing quicker and more shallowly than usual. He was getting too tense. He tried to relax. He forced himself to watch the rabbits. He singled out a small one with a white blaze down its front. There was something pleasant, innocent about it. He watched it intently…

2

The camp had been easy. The guards were for the most part young and raw, and there weren't very many of them. Then they might have expected trouble from inside, but not from outside. At five to six they had cut their way through the wire. The circle of lights that ringed the camp at night had been cut off and they had worked in the deep shadows at the wire unseen from the tall, wooden-legged observation towers at each corner of the camp. Once inside they had split up into four groups, two putting the guard-room and the two nearest towers out of action, while the remaining two groups had begun to open the doors to the huts. Before the guards had realized what had happened the camp was almost taken.

Now from the four corners of the camp they came running, filthy, ragged, with shaven heads, shouting and screaming, towards the earthen square, regardless of the sporadic rifle-fire from the remaining two towers. Here and there a man was brought down to the ground, but his comrades ran on, without even pausing. They pressed round Krause and his men and the group of fur-capped guards, some still in their underwear, and clamoured for information.

'Wer seid Ihr?'

'Was wollt Ihr?'

'Ist der Kreig ausgebrochen?'

The old man tried to tell them what to do, but he could not make himself heard above the noise. Over and over again they repeated the same questions stupidly whilst he bellowed the answers at them.

'We want you to go, lads!' he shouted. 'Get away from here straight off. Don't bother about your things if you have any. Straight off!'

But no one seemed to take any notice.

A man with a scar from his eye to the edge of his mouth pushed his way through the shouting mob. He had one hand pressed to his shoulder. His fingers and shirt were bloodstained.

'Are you wounded?' the old man asked, concerned.

'It is of no importance,' the man said. His eyes sparkled light and high on the eyeball, like the old man remembered men's eyes sparkling in the brothels behind the front in the old war.

The old man repeated his question, but the man ignored him. He pushed Krause to one side and forced his way through to the Russians. Mostly they were in their teens, their uniforms badly-fitting and very loose at the necks, looking, with their shaven heads, almost as starved as their prisoners. The man pushed them to one side as if they were animals, until he stood face to face with a man much older than the rest. He was dressed in breeches and jackboots, his chest bare. Beneath his left breast there was the deep, gnarled pit of an old wound. He was already grey at the temples.

'Report Sergeant-Major!' the man bellowed and slapped the Russian across the face.

The man staggered, but didn't lose his smile. 'Ne ponimyu,' he said softly.

'You understand all right, you swine!' the man shouted, and struck the Russian with his clenched fist. The blow caught the Russian directly on the mouth. His face went deadly white and then the spaces between his teeth began to fill rapidly with blood.

The old man forced his way across to the prisoner and took his arm just as he was going to strike the Russian again.

'You can't do this,' he said gently. 'Please forget now.'

'Forget!' the little man shouted and swung himself free. 'Can I forget this?' He pointed to the scar on his face. 'Or this?' He held the bloody palm of his other hand under Krause's nose.

Without waiting for an answer, he hit the Russian again with his good hand. He struck his nose. Something crunched and the Russian swayed back on his heels. Dark red blood started to pour from his nostrils.

But still he retained his grimace of a smile.

'Report Sergeant-Major! Report, you bastard, like you made us report!'

Someone in the crowd fell wounded by the bullets of the Russians in the towers, and the crowd set up a howl. 'Don't waste time, Max! Kill the swine! Kill all of them!'

'Give me room, then!' Max bellowed above the roar. He turned quickly and pulled at the old man's rifle. The old man held firm. The little man put his foot in Krause's stomach and he rolled backwards in the dirt. With a backward swing of his new rifle, the little man warned the crowd to keep behind him. Instinctively the Russians edged away; all except the sergeant-major. He stood there, his head held high, facing the little man.

Holding the butt of the rifle in his thigh, bending slightly to do so, the little man pointed it at the Russian.

'Now. Comrade Bastard, are you going to report?'

'Ne ponimyu!' The sergeant-major said thickly, licking at the blood that fell from his nose before he could speak.

'I shall give you three to report.'

The Russian did not say anything.

'One, two, three,' the little man counted

slowly, and the lips of the crowd moved silently with him. Then he fired. The rifle jerked violently, and he had difficulty holding it. The bullet missed the Russian, sending up a spurt of dust a few metres away from him. The crowd, which had fallen silent, started shouting again, but the sergeant-major silenced them suddenly with a shout. 'Ruhe – Quiet!' Then softly in good German he said. 'This', – he pointed at the hole under the taut nipple of his breast – 'you did last time. Now you wish to finish it.' He addressed his words to the little man. 'Aim at this. It will be easier.'

Hurriedly the little man put the muzzle of his rifle on the toe of his boot, pulled back the bolt and ejected the spent cartridge and loaded again.

'Here,' the Russian said, placing his finger on the scar, but not taking his eyes off the little man.

'There!' the little man almost screamed, and rammed the muzzle of the rifle deep into the old wound so that the Russian staggered. A drop of blood fell from the man's nose on to the stock of the rifle. The little man clenched his hand on the butt. The Russian looked at him for the last time and then focused his eyes on some spot above the little man's head away in the distance.

He fired, and the Russian flew back into the dust; the front of his chest gone. The old man, supported by one of the others, looked away. The spell was broken. A deep throaty roar went up from the crowd. They ran forward and threw themselves on the guards, beating them with their bare fists and here and there the butt of a captured rifle. Then men started to break away from the crowd and ran into the guard-room, to reappear a few moments later with small cans of petrol.

One suddenly began to run for the towers, crouched low, the heavy can bumping against his legs awkwardly as he ran in zig-zags to avoid the fire from the towers. Then he was hit and went down, the contents of his can splashing out two metres or so in front of him on to the dry ground. Another followed him. He passed the body in the dust and then abruptly he stopped, clutched his knee, clapped up one of his hands and stared stupidly at the blood and began to cry. A moment later a second bullet flung him down on his face. He didn't move this time. A third prisoner was only hit when he was within a few metres of the base of the nearest tower. The crowd were suddenly tired of beating the guards. The new game interested them more. In a moment everyone was fighting to obtain one of the cans of petrol. A good half-dozen men sprinted across the open space to the tower, urged on by the shouts of their comrades. It was almost like a crowd at a football match.

The first one fell. Then another. And another. One fell within a metre of the base of the tower. He raised himself up on his elbows and splashed the contents of his can forward. The man behind him crouched down, oblivious to the bullets striking up little spurts of dust on the ground around him, struck a match and threw it forward into the trail of petrol. A blue line ran towards the tower for a second and then there was a dull bang, followed by the inward sucking of air, and the base of the tower went up in flames.

A great roar burst from the crowd, and abruptly the firing from the tower stopped. Quickly the flames mounted upwards.

A moment later the other tower was reached, but as the first man there fumbled with his matches, he was hit and fell grasping at his throat. Suddenly one of the young Russians of the guard forced his way through the watching prisoners. His broad peasant face was covered in an excited grin, in spite of his blackened, swollen eye and bruised cheek.

'I go, please. I go,' he said in broken German.

'Did you hear that?' they said.

'Please I go,' he pleaded.

'Yes, go,' they said. 'Yes.'

And before they could stop him, he was running in a zigzag, crouched double, his thin wrists sticking out from his too-short jacket. He seemed to bear a charmed life. The men in the remaining tower started firing in earnest as soon as they realized what he was going to do. But in spite of their concentrated firing he reached the base of the tower, and waving with one hand to the crowd, lit the petrol with the other.

The crowd surged forward, shouting, to the tower, waving the planks torn from their bunks. Firing had ceased now. The tower was almost obscured by thick black smoke.

'Burn the swine! Burn the swine!' they shouted as they ran forward.

The old man and the men with him watched them go. He felt sickened. He knew these things happened. He had seen similar things in the war long ago. He felt like running and hiding himself so that he would

186

never have to see a human being again. He was an old man, and old men don't vomit easily. But it would have been easy for him then.

'What can we do to stop them?' he asked the men around him.

But they were silent, their eyes embarrassed and downcast, as if they had been caught in the lonely pleasures of youth. At the tower a soldier was pushing his leg through the broken window and looking down at the smoke, panic-stricken. At the sight of him another roar went up from the crowd and they started throwing stones up at him. The soldier screamed high and harsh. Then the smoke obscured him from their view. One of the remaining Russians went white and began to cry, staring straight ahead, the tears trickling down his cheeks unnoticed. The others huddled together like animals, their heads hunched in their shoulders instinctively, expecting blows.

'Come on, Ewald. There is no purpose in staying here.' One of his comrades took him by the arm and the old man let himself be led.

'Du hast recht, Rudi.' Then he paused and crooked his finger at the Russians to come. He pointed at the gate.

'Idyut! Davei!' he said, remembering the words from almost forty years before. 'Davoi! Los!'

The Russians began to run, their hands clasped over the backs of their shaven heads, still expecting further blows. The old man watched them through the gate and then nodded to the others. 'Let us go back now.'

Behind them the legs of the tower cracked sharp, like a bone breaking. A shower of sparks curved into the morning air and disappeared into the flames. Slowly the tower trembled, bent, and then crashed to the ground.

3

The truck was coming now. It was old and moved slowly. The technicians stood crowded together in the back and they were singing. It was a fine morning and they were singing. It didn't sound like one of the Party songs. Without turning his head, Richard asked the fat man what they were singing. But the fat man did not answer. Richard screwed his head round and squinted at him. The fat man was sweating heavily, his eyes staring along his rifle aimed at the road and seeing nothing.

Richard looked down at the road again. The truck had turned the bend and the rabbits scattered, except the one with the white blaze. It moved backwards a few paces and hunched, staring stupidly at the on-coming truck. Richard's hands, which had instinctively tightened on the plunger, relaxed sweatily, and he stared at the rabbit as if hypnotized. The truck came on steadily. At the back of his brain a little voice was saying, 'Now-now-now'. Suddenly the rabbit turned and began to run, straight and in the centre of the road, instead of into the verges. Richard clenched his free fist. 'On to the verge, the verge, you bloody fool!' he cursed to himself in English. Then, before he really realized he was doing it, he pressed the plunger.

The road roared to life violently under the cab of the old truck. The vehicle rose into the air like a wave breaking against a cliff. Then a ball of red in a cloud of yellow, which became black almost at once. The hills threw back the dull thunder, and if there were screams, Richard didn't hear them. He pressed his head, cradled in his arms, to the ground, and it came up to meet him. A moment later a rain of pebbles and clods of earth hit the ground all round him.

Quickly he released the plunger and began pumping shot after shot into the smoke. A blackened figure fell out of the smoke. For a moment it stood there puzzled, looking from side to side, then it started to run. It ran clumsily down the centre of the road in a stumbling jog-trot. Very carefully, aiming slightly off for the wind, finger smooth on the trigger for the first pressure, even movement in the second, Richard fired, and the man fell. He stopped firing, and after a few more shots the others did too.

Richard watched the truck intently. The volume of the smoke had lessened and, a thin, oily black, it went almost straight up into the still morning air. There was no movement now.

'Die haben's erwischt,' he said to the fat man, screwing his neck round.

But the fat man did not answer. He was still staring blankly along his rifle.

'You,' Richard said sharply and gave him a dig in the ribs.

The fat man rolled over on his back and his mouth fell open stupidly. Like ripening plums, his nails flooded a rosy-blue. He was dead.

Richard looked him over quickly. There were no marks or wounds that he could see. But he was dead all right. He got up and slung the fat man's rifle over his shoulder, and carrying his machine-pistol he ran down through the trees towards the road. He could see the others running from the hiding-places around the road. Richard ran a little faster. For some reason or other he wanted to be at the truck before they arrived. He didn't want anyone else but himself to be first on the road.

There was no sign of the rabbit with the white blaze. He looked at the truck and felt no emotion. They were dead, and in death they had lost all their power to wake emotion in him.

The others came up, red-faced and panting from the recent exertion. They were middle-aged like the rest that had set out that morning. They were no longer the stuff that soldiers were supposed to be made of, but they were doing well for all that, Richard thought.

'That you did well,' he said. 'Very well.'

They said nothing. One of them began to turn a body over with the toe of his boot. The others looked at him sharply, and he pulled his foot away quickly.

191

'The fat man is dead,' Richard said. 'I don't know how it happened. There was no mark on him. Perhaps he had a weak heart.'

An old man in a leather coat shook his head. 'No, he hadn't, Ami. Paul was a coward. Remember him as a coward when we were at school together. Never would fight anybody like the other lads.'

Richard realized again what an impossible adventure these men were undertaking.

From behind the trees there came the sound of rifle-fire, punctuated by the heavier burr of a machine-gun. There was no mistaking the sound this time. It was the factory. The five of them ran back to where their bicycles were hidden in the ditch. As they ran it started to rain – at first slowly and at intervals; then quicker. Great heavy drops that hit the road with a hiss and spattered out the size of a Taler. Steam began to rise from the truck. Suddenly the smoke from its burnt interior stopped. The rain they had been expecting for so long had come at last...

CHAPTER THIRTEEN

Behind them their truck was crashed crazily into the wooden guard-room at the gate, the rear-side door hanging on by one hinge, both windows starred and splintered. Round about lay the bodies of the guard, some clad only in their boots and under-clothes. In the middle of the road lay a dog, its fur ragged and sodden by the rain that pelted down and made the gutters noisy.

They lay in the rain, which beat down savagely on the concrete of the yard, splashing up and outwards again in little sprays, and watched Von Kornfeld. Their clothes clung blackly to their soaked backs. Von Kornfeld was farthest forward of them all, sprawled full length in the centre of the yard behind the body of one of the boilermen. His feet were turned outwards, and from where they lay they could see the hole in the sole of his left boot.

The rain fell in a white sheet in front of their eyes and sprayed upwards from the concrete and struck them warmly in the face. Somehow they felt they couldn't die in the rain. You didn't die in the rain. Then a vicious burr and a burst of fire along their front from the machine-gun in the shed reminded them that they could. They sucked in their stomachs and felt themselves sink into the earth. It was as if they were making love to a woman when they were young. But they weren't young and they didn't make love any more.

Suddenly it seemed silly to them that they should be lying there, like boys playing games. They were 'solide Buerger', with grown families and responsibilities. This wasn't for them. In a moment, they told themselves, they would get up and run for shelter out of the rain which was soaking them to the skin and would probably give them pneumonia. Another burst of machine-gun fire sent angry, fiery-red sparks up from the concrete in front of them, and they hugged the earth as if they were wedded to it.

Von Kornfeld waved his arm to the left and then to the right, and it all came back to them from the times in the French mud of forty years before. And they got up and made the desperate series of doubled, lung-bursting, heart-pounding dashes for the flanks. Von Kornfeld raised himself a little and bullets thudded dully into the body in front and heaved at it, as if trying to turn it over. He ducked down again. He had seen what he had wanted to see. There was only one of them. He had the M.G. 42 in the corner of the shed. The belt with its two hundred and fifty rounds was nearly finished.

'Fire!' he shouted to the men on his left. 'Fire at him!'

A volley of bullets rattled harmlessly against the corrugated metal of the shed. The gun turned in their direction and scythed the air terrifyingly. Then Von Kornfeld was up and running towards the shed. The fire turned on him. Something struck his boot. He stumbled, righted himself and ran on again. He was banking on the man's inexperience of this kind of direct attack. Otherwise what he was doing was madness – for any normal man, he told himself. For any normal man.

The gun coughed – stopped – fired again – coughed and stopped. Von Kornfeld had a jolted, blurred picture of the man in front of him. The policeman, his face sweaty and filthy, a black ring of beard round his mouth, backed against the wall of the shed, his eyes big and staring at Von Kornfeld, his hand grasping stupidly for the empty holster at his belt. Von Kornfeld shot him as he ran at two metres distance and then collided with him, as he doubled up and fell face forward. For the fraction of a second he had a glimpse of a crumbled face full of pain and surprise, and then he, too, fell to the floor on top of the man. He lay there panting for a moment, feeling the life go out of the man underneath, whilst he fought with it and the air bubbled bloodily through his lungs and then it was over: the man lay still.

It seemed a long time before he could make himself get up. Everywhere there was silence now. Suddenly the rain stopped and the men came into the sheds from the flanks, their weapons still held at the ready. The factory was theirs.

2

Richard pushed his bicycle up the wet, shining road to the factory with his four riflemen. His hair was plastered damply to his forehead and he had the rifle of the dead man slung over his shoulder; his machine-pistol he held over the handle-bars of his bicycle. Down below in the town there was still the thin crackle of fire from the direction of the barracks, but the crowds that had been ransacking the State shops and offices on the mainstreet had now disappeared. On the top of the hill there was no sound.

They edged their way past the truck that blocked the entrance to the factory and stepped over the bodies. The men with him looked at them curiously.

'That's Heinz's lad,' the old man in the leather coat said pointing at one of them.

'Is it?' someone asked.

'Yes. I've known him since he was quite small. Couldn't mistake him.'

They went on, and then they saw the others, squatting on their heels, rifles between their wide-spread knees, or leaning against the wall, rifles slung over their shoulders. Richard saw the old man and Von Kornfeld and hurried over to them.

The old man still looked stern, but his eyes were shining with success. He stretched out his hand. Richard thrust his out and the old man pressed it hard.

'We've done it,' he said joyfully. 'We're in now.' He looked at Richard's four riflemen. 'And how was it with you?'

'Good. We had one man dead.'

'Who?'

'A fat man. He sweated a great deal.'

'Ellerbrock. I know him.'

'And you?' Richard asked. 'How did it go with you? Good?'

'Two men wounded – lightly,' the old man answered.

'And you?' Richard looked at Von Kornfeld.

'None. We were lucky. One or two of the boilermen, of course. But that was to be expected,' Von Kornfeld said conversationally.

'It was to be expected.' Richard echoed his words.

Von Kornfeld lit a cigarette and they chatted a while.

'What do we do now?' the old man asked Richard.

'You have prepared for them when they come?' Richard asked.

'Yes.'

Richard shrugged his shoulders. 'Then there is nothing. Nothing now but to wait.'

Von Kornfeld nodded. 'Yes, just wait. It was always so. A little fighting and a lot of waiting.'

The three of them laughed drily and then suddenly the laughter died on Richard's face.

Across from one of the sheds he saw the girl coming towards him. When she saw him, she stopped for a fraction of a second and then started running.

'I couldn't stop her,' he heard Von Kornfeld say miles away. 'She came with us in the truck. I could do nothing to stop her. I am truly sorry...'

And then she was in his arms, warm and panting, her body melting into his. 'Thou art safe! Thou art safe, Richard!'

With his free hand he ruffled her hair. 'Of course, little one. What didst thou expect?'

She went red, conscious suddenly of the eyes of the men on her, and released herself from his grasp.

'Thou art foolish to have come, Stine,' he said severely, but inside his heart was light that she had come. 'It were better if thou hadst stayed at home.'

Her face grew soft. 'Please, Richard, do not be angry with me. It is too late now.'

He smiled, and her face became bright again.

From the direction of the town there came the thick, leaden beat of a heavy machine-gun. But the pauses between its bursts were still punctuated by the steady, clear sharpness of rifle-fire.

'They're still at it,' the old man said, turning his head to the sound. 'They're good lads – the both of them.'

'The snipers?' Richard asked.

'Yes. Before the war they used to be champion shots hereabout. Once they even went to Berlin for a competition.'

They listened again, but if the rifles were still firing, they were obscured now by the patient, relentless boring of the machine-gun.

The old man in the leather coat came across to them in a breathless half-run.

'Ewald,' he shouted excitedly, while he was still some distance away. 'They've started some trouble in Berlin.'

Everyone turned to listen to him as he panted out his news. 'I've been listening to the N.W.D.R. from Hamburg. In the radio. Over there – in the hut – the guard-room.'

'Get on with it,' somebody shouted.

'Give me a chance,' the old man panted.

'Well, they said on the radio that they've begun a big strike in Berlin and our lot have marched up to the Potsdamer Platz and that way, and … they've burnt stores and things down. The Vopos rushed 'em, but the fellow in the wireless says the Vopos are losing control and Ivan's just standing there and watching the Vopos get a skin-full.'

'Did you hear that, lads?' the old man shouted. 'Now it's starting!'

Everywhere the tired, strained faces of the men relaxed happily. They came to life again.

Richard looked at their happy faces and he, too, let himself believe that they might be successful.

'Wait till old Conrad's pinning that big medal on thee in Bonn!' somebody shouted happily.

'Thou canst kiss me where I am beautiful and have no nose.'

In the noise and excited chatter no one noticed that the firing from the direction of the town had stopped.

CHAPTER FOURTEEN

They moved at high speed from the barracks, the tyres of the trucks in convoy hissing smoothly over the wet macadam. There were four trucks, each containing twenty wet policemen, their helmets gleaming in the watery sun that was trying to break through the clouds, their rifles clasped between their knees.

It had taken them two hours to get out of the barracks after the first alarm, and it had cost them two men killed and eight wounded before they had been able to rush the wooded hill and kill the two of them.

The convoy turned into the main streets and the trucks skidded one after another to a wild stop, one of them mounting the pavement and narrowly missing a lamp-post.

A man lay in the dirt. He lay on his back and stared with glassy eyes at the sky. The man was dead. A man in brown overalls that shopkeepers wear, and no shoes. Wagner noticed automatically that he had a hole in his left sock. It was Stutz, the manager of the State shop.

Wagner got out of the cab of the first truck and undid the flap of his revolver holster. As far as he could see the street was littered with paper and broken glass. Not one of the windows around him was intact. The whole length of the street towards the factory lay in a thick, feeling silence. He crunched his way across broken glass, resisting a sudden urge to go on tip-toe, to the State shop.

Smoke poured thinly through the shattered window into the damp air. He put his foot to the crazily-hanging door and kicked it in. It fell noisily into the broken glass, and back in the truck someone made a frightened, suppressed noise.

Wagner glared angrily. A young policeman went red and glanced down at his hands holding the rifle. Wagner looked inside the shop. The place was littered like the street, and in the centre of the floor a heap of empty shoe-boxes smouldered. Everywhere the drawers hung open, some of their contents hanging out and others strewn down on the counters. In the corner there was a heap of new stockings, and he wondered idly for a moment why no one had taken them. Otherwise the place had been plundered well and truly, he told himself. He turned and crunched his way back to the truck. His men looked at him expectantly.

'A section out of every truck!' he shouted, 'and a bit sharpish.'

Obediently the young policemen began to drop over the sides of the trucks into the litter, holding their rifles up above their heads as they did so.

'Section One over on the pavement on the left. That's right – hug the wall!' Wagner swung his arm round to the opposite pavement. 'Section Two over there. About ten metres behind them. And Section Three fall in at the rear!'

He turned to the men remaining in the trucks. 'You men keep your eyes on the top-storey windows. Anything moves, give 'em it quick. We don't want to spend another two hours over snipers!'

Wagner stepped on to the cab of the first truck and crooked his arm through the window, his feet on the running-board. 'Distance of ten metres between vehicles!' he shouted to the next truck. He nodded to his driver. 'Right, off you go. Second gear, and watch what you're doing.'

They moved forward bumpily over the littered street. In front of the school the road was covered with sodden text-books. Wagner caught a glimpse of a Marx illustration. Then the driver swerved to avoid going over a flag spread in the middle of the road. Formerly it had hung before the school, but now it was spread out in the middle of the road. Someone had used it for a purpose it had never been intended for. At the back of the truck somebody giggled nervously. Wagner turned and looked back at them steadily. The giggling stopped.

They were half way up the street now. Wagner could see the truck crashed into the gate of the factory quite clearly.

'Comrade Captain!' somebody shouted.

He looked down at Number One Section. The section-leader was pointing at a figure lying in the gutter of an alley running off the main street. Wagner recognized the figure at once: by the gloves.

He dropped off the running-board and ran ahead of the truck to where the section-leader stood.

It was Todt all right. One glass of his new pince-nez was a splintered, bloody hole. His white gloved hand lay stained in the dirty water that flowed down the gutter to the grate. The flaps of his jacket had been thrown up and his pockets searched. The dirty white linings of his pockets stood stiffly in the air. His pistol was missing too. Wagner looked down at him for a moment and then nodded to the section-leader. He wasn't particularly sorry that Todt was gone. He ran back to the truck and signalled to the driver to carry on.

They arrived at the foot of the hill. The men of the leading two sections spread out instinctively and the Number One Section-Leader looked back over his shoulder. Wagner waved him on. Wagner's driver fumbled with his gears, changing down to first, and Wagner cursed him. At that moment Number One Section came under fire. It was ragged but effective. The section's reaction was good, but they left two of their number on the ground.

Wagner reached through, grabbed the wheel of his truck and swung it round, blocking the road. He dropped off the running-board and waved for Number Two Section to take cover. Everywhere the policemen were dropping into the wet grass alongside the road, body in the correct position at a forty-five-degree angle to their rifle. A bullet hit the ground a metre from him and Wagner flung himself to the ground quickly.

The section-leader of Number One Section crawled over to him. On his arm he had a tourniquet made of his black tie and a pencil. He was deadly pale.

'Two men stopped one, Comrade Captain,' he said.

Wagner nodded impatiently, his eyes on the top of the hill. 'Yes, I saw. And your arm?'

'Nothing of importance at the moment. Shall I take my lot up against the bastards?'

'No,' Wagner said sharply. 'There'll be no more killing this day.'

'What are you going to do then, Comrade Captain? There is no other way, as far as I can see.'

'There is. I know these brothers up on the hill. I went to school with most of them, worked with a lot of 'em. Man, if they'll listen to anybody, they'll listen to me.' He stuck the stump of an unlit cigar in his mouth and pulled out a white handkerchief. He got up and the section-leader grabbed at his arm. 'Don't do it, Captain. They'll slaughter you.'

Wagner knocked his arm away.

'Stop firing, everybody!' Wagner bellowed to left and then to right. 'I'm going up the hill!'

He started walking up the wet road, pressing his heels against the concrete, cap stuck at the back of his head, the unlit cigar between his lips. Half way up he lowered the handkerchief he was waving above his head and stuck his hands on his hips in his favourite pose. The firing from the factory stopped.

'Listen!' Wagner shouted. 'It's me, Wagner! You know me, lads! Big Wagner!' He took a great gulp of air. 'You, Max Klein! You, Toni Grunwald! You, Ewald Krause! You all know me! You've known me all your life! We went to school together! We went out with the same girls! We got drunk together! We've worked together! I'm not one of your fine pees! I'm one of you lads, and you know it!'

The old man glanced up from behind the wall and watched the faces of the men around him. Suddenly they had grown uncertain. A kind of shyness unnatural in men their age had veiled their eyes.

'It's Big Wagner,' someone whispered, as if he had made a discovery. 'Tell him a mile off, with that cigar stuck in his face!'

'That's right. Big Wagner.'

The policeman was shouting again, and the old man turned to listen.

'This is what I've got to say to you, lads! You've done bad things today, some of you! You've burnt and you've killed and you've fought against your country! And you'll have to be punished for it! I'm telling you straight! There are no two ways about it! You've got to be punished! But everybody makes mistakes! We all do!' Wagner had started moving forward again, his hands in his pockets. 'Remember that time, Max Klein, when you got drunk and smashed up Jaegersbrunnen? And you, Toni Grunwald. Do you remember how you beat up that S.A. man? You had to pay then. I had to pay with you. Both of us had to! And you'll pay this time! But I promise you this!' He paused. He was quite close now. And his eyes swept the blank wall in front of him. 'I promise you this! If you come out now, with no further trouble, it'll be a lot better for you than if we have to come up and fetch you! Come out, lads, and take your punishment, rather than make us come and get you – dead!'

The old man didn't need to look round. He could feel their reaction in the air. They didn't need to say anything. He could feel it. This was Big Wagner, they were thinking. We've known him since we were kids together. He's not trying to hang one on us. Perhaps if we stopped now– Suddenly the old man cupped his hands together and shouted. 'Listen, Wagner. With you and your kind we don't want anything to do! Now get yourself down that hill quick, or you're a dead man!'

'Is that you, Ewald?' Wagner shouted, the butt of his cigar stuck to his upper lip.

The old man didn't say anything.

'Ewald, sie doch vernunftig! – be reasonable! You know me! I'm not telling any fairytales! Believe me–'

'Stop the air! And get back where you came from!'

'But, Ewald, listen to reason! I'm one of you, aren't I?'

'You're not one of us, Wagner! You haven't been one of us for years. Go on – quick!'

But Wagner did not go. He stood there, puzzled and persistent. The old man knew then that he would have to shoot him. He looked once more at the living man: cap at the back of his head, lock of black hair hanging down at the front, cigar stuck to his upper lip; legs spread apart firmly, securely apart. It was a body built for fun. He remembered Wagner as a child in the little white apron with pockets at the front that children wore in those days to go to school. It was summer, and he had wanted to go to school barefoot, like all the other children, and he had stood there in front of his mother as he stood there now. The old man took careful aim and fired. The shot went low. Wagner fell on one knee, and even at that distance the old man could see the look of amazement on his face.

Wagner struggled for a moment, then, with a great effort, he rose to his feet again and staggered forward, his big hands grabbing at the air, as if he were pulling himself along by invisible hand-holds.

Mechanically the old man ejected the spent cartridge and aimed again. His sight blurred and he blinked his eyes quickly. His vision cleared again and he was alone with Wagner and the world. He squeezed the trigger evenly. The bullet hit Wagner squarely and savagely in the stomach, and the old man could almost feel the shot strike into the taut flesh. Slowly the big man toppled forward, shouting. And his words seemed to hang on the air for a long time after the echo of the shot had died away. 'But it's me, Ewald. Me, Big Wagner.'

And then they were coming up the hill, black and young, shouting their 'hurrahs' as they had been taught to do in their training-schools. But their instructors had been men who were used to the resources of a nation whose man-power was cheap and inexhaustible, and they had never been taught to spread out evenly and thinly. The old man remembered the times at Tannenberg when even after he had closed his eyes and fired, sick of the slaughter, he could not help killing them. He fired again and again, feeling the butt pound back against his shoulder until it became sore. The whole line of the factory-wall erupted into fire against the advancing line of black. And it was like no firing-line the old man had ever experienced. There were none of the curses and the deep animal grunts of pleasure at the killing. For these men dying were their sons and the sons of their sons.

They were fifty – forty – thirty metres away. The old man could see them swallowing the dry spit in their throats as they ran, gasping for breath. Then they were twenty metres away. They were falling all along the line, without even being able to fire back at the high, blank wall. They wavered. There and there and there a man looked to see where his neighbour was. And then suddenly they had turned and were running back the way they had come, dropping their rifles as they ran, fighting for position in their panic-stricken attempts to get down the hill and out of the hail of bullets.

Number One Section-Leader, who had been wounded again in the thigh, sat and levelled his revolver at them. 'Stop!' he shouted. 'Stop where you are!' but they ran on and passed him, his threats ignored. Slowly he dropped his revolver and watched them run unbelievingly.

At the wall the fire gradually slackened and then died away altogether. And in the stupidness that comes after battle when the deafening roar of concentrated firing cuts you off from the outside and imprisons you in a little world of your own, they held their rifles by the red-hot muzzles and burnt themselves, put cigarettes in their mouths, lit matches and blew them out again, without even applying them to the ends of the cigarettes. And then, after only a few moments, they wanted to see their handi-work again and peered out from the wall across the hill.

There was no movement now except for the section-leader, who sat there swaying slightly from side to side, staring blankly at the wall. They could see the blood staining his breeches and he had relaxed his hold on the tourniquet, which was slowly, very slowly unwinding itself. He stared up at them till they could stand it no longer.

'Get yourself off, man,' someone shouted hoarsely. 'We won't hurt yer!'

'Yes, go on now and get that arm seen to!' someone else added.

The second-leader came out of his doze. He tried to rise, but failed and sank down again.

'The carbine next to you!' the old man in the leather coat shouted. 'Use that to get yourself up!'

The man reached out for the carbine and levered himself with its aid. And then, using it as a crutch, hobbled slowly and painfully down the road.

CHAPTER FIFTEEN

Alongside the whole wall of the room there were the ruins of a buffet, the stained white tablecloth hanging down askew almost to the floor, with its pools of spilled wine. The great bare fireplace was already full of broken, splintered glasses, and one or two of them had missed the fireplace and splattered the wall with their contents. The air was thick with blue strong tobacco smoke.

The men in the corner held themselves stiffly – almost at attention – and waited, trying to ignore the drunken life and noise around them. In the centre of the room a fat man, naked to the waist, with the red-striped breeches of a senior officer, was being prepared for the stick. With a grunt he sat down and pulled his knees up to his chin. A stick was pushed through his bended knees. He put his arms round it and clasped his hands so that the stick lay tightly between his knees and elbows. Then his hands were strapped together with a leather strap and two men with the broad golden epaulets of a major lifted him up by the ends of the stick, which they propped up on two tables.

The general stood with his back to them, stop-watch in hand. 'Now!' he barked.

And the two majors began to rotate the fat man on the stick like a wheel. Faster and faster. The fat man's head missed the floor by inches.

The general raised the forefinger of his right hand, his eyes fixed on the watch, and then he brought his hand down sharply. 'Enough!' he shouted.

Quickly the two majors lowered the stick and untied the strap.

The fat man staggered and would have sunk to his knees if the two majors had not caught him in time.

'Point him at the drink!' the general said excitedly.

The two majors turned the fat man until he faced the table some six feet away, upon which stood a bottle. Then they let go. The fat man sank to his knees and then got to his feet again. His eyes bulged from his head and his face was brick-red, as if he were going to have a stroke. He reached out a shaky hand and took a step forward. The next moment he fell down flat on his face.

Everyone laughed, and the general was the first in the rush to pick him up. He lifted him as if he were no weight at all.

'Ivan Ilyvitch, thou art truly nothing of a man!' he roared, his face red with laughter at the stupid dazed look on the fat man's face. 'Thou art not the man thou wert, little brother!'

The fat man wiped the sweat from his brow with a shaky hand and shook his head several times before he could drink the glass of vodka the general offered him.

The men standing stiffly in the corner tried to catch the general's eye but he ignored them, although, they told themselves, he knew full well that they had been there a good hour already. The general unbuckled his belt and ripped down the buttons of his tight tunic. Pulling it off, he threw it at the fat colonel. 'Here, little brother!' he shouted. 'Hold this. Now thou wilt see a real man do it!'

In trying to catch the tunic, the fat colonel upset his drink over his bare stomach, and he jumped at the shock of the cold liquid. Everyone laughed.

The men in the corner watched the squat, powerful figure of the general being tied to the stick, but they were apart from the room, cold and reserved, and their eyes showed none of the interest or excitement of the others. They waited now, they told themselves. They waited today, but their turn would come – it always did.

General Telegin was the youngest of the field-officers in the room, and yet he commanded the crack division of the Army of Occupation. The story of his rise to fame was like one of those stories from the days of the Civil War. In June 1941 he had been a tractor driver on a Kolkhoz in the Western Ukraine – a seventeen-year-old who could hardly read or write, his only claim to fame being that he had sired more illegitimate children than any other boy of his age in the village.

Then the Germans came. Within a week they had swept through his village and occupied territory a hundred and fifty kilometers to the east. Within four weeks the tractor driver had organized a partisan unit of his own in the forest and was already harassing the German lines of communication.

A year later he was one of the best-known partisan leaders in the Western Ukraine. For two years he fought in the swamps and forests of his homeland, until in 1943 he was called into the Red Army.

Here he learnt his theory as he put it into practice. He didn't scorn the regulation issue of eighty text-books for officers, but he opened them and examined his tactics after he had successfully carried out the tactic. He went up the ladder of rank quickly – there were always plenty of vacancies in the Third Ukraine Army. Tolbukin's officers didn't last long. He became one of the heroes of the Soviet Union. The first tank lieutenant to outfight a Tiger in a T.34. The captain whose troop of light tanks ambushed and decimated half a German regiment. The major whose reconnaissance in force became virtually a minor offensive.

At the end of the war he was a regimental commander and a Hero of the Soviet Union. And now at thirty he was General commanding the 'Iron Division', the best tank division in the Red Army, and in consequence of that, as his officers said, the best tank division in the World.

He was a typical Ukrainian. Small and very broad-shouldered, with the thick, broad neck, large nose and shaven, pear-shaped head. In spite of his high spirits and heavy humour there always lingered something sad and unfulfilled about his glance and the way his lips drooped at the corners:

it was the look of the peasant who knows he'll always be a peasant, for all the work he does.

They had spun the general, unlashed his hands and pointed him in the direction of the bottle. He stood for a moment, swaying slightly, and then stepped forward. His foot slipped from under him, and it looked as if he were going to fall. But he righted and headed for the bottle, zig-zagging from side to side, a stupid grin on his red face. He made it and grabbed the edge of the table to prevent himself from falling.

'Salt!' he shouted. 'The salt!'

A young officer rushed forward with a saucer full of salt.

Concentrating hard, the general took a large pinch between his thick, stubby forefinger and thumb and put it on the back of his hand. Then, wetting his lips he licked it and raised the bottle to his lips. He drank deeply while the white liquid trickled down over his chest, until his breath went. With a crack he set the bottle down on the table again and stood there swaying, gasping for breath.

Everyone clapped and applauded noisily. The general smiled triumphantly, and let the liquor drip down his chin on to his shirt without making any attempt to stop it.

'You, old men. That's the way we do it in the Iron Division,' he said thickly.

'One day your heart will stop on that stick, Comrade General,' the fat man said.

'One day my heart will stop anyway, little brother.' The general laughed and clapped the fat man on the back.

The men in the corner could wait no longer. The three of them pushed their way through the crowd round the general without apologies, knocking aside officers, who were much senior to themselves in rank. But the protests of the offended men died on their lips when they saw the purple rings on the caps that the three men carried under their arms. They were officers of the M.V.D. The general watched them push their way through the crowd in silence. They introduced themselves briskly.

'Comrade General, we are officers of the M.V.D. attached to a unit of People's Armed Forces of the People's Republic,' their spokesman said, a tall, thin captain, who looked more like a school-teacher than a soldier.

A typical Politiruk officer – political officer – the general thought. He'd seen them often enough during the war – always before an action and after one, but never in one, as the troops used to say.

The general acknowledged their introductions with a slight bow, but still said nothing.

'Comrade General, we have been waiting here to see you for one hour – one whole hour,' the tall captain emphasized the words expressly. It was supposed to be a warning.

'I know you have,' the general said calmly. 'I saw you come in.'

The captain pulled a face. 'May I inquire, then, Comrade General, why you have kept us waiting? You realize that we don't come here for our own pleasure at this time of the night.'

General Telegin looked at the captain steadily for a long time. 'First of all, Captain, you don't ask generals questions; and secondly, wipe that look off your face. You look as if you've done it in your pants!' He said the words loudly, so that the people in the room couldn't but hear them.

The officers present were embarrassed. One didn't speak to the M.V.D. like that. Or at least not more than once – even if they were several ranks below you and you were a general.

The tall captain went red and then white.

One could see that he had never been spoken to like this before.

'I'm Telegin of the Iron Division,' the general went on. 'Mark the name. Everybody knows me all over Russia from Moscow to places you've never heard of, Captain.' He poked himself in the chest. 'I'm a Hero of the Soviet Union. I'm their hero. I've the best division in the army. Me, I'll be Chief of Staff in ten years' time. So you and your kind can't frighten me, brother. And don't think you ever will!' The last sentences he delivered in his native Ukrainian, and the captain, who spoke as if he came from Russia, flushed again.

The general clicked his thick fingers together loudly, and the young officer, who had brought the salt, came forward again with a glass in his hand.

Telegin drained it in a gulp and then threw it accurately into the fireplace, where it shattered against the brick. 'That's the kind of man I am, Comrade Captain,' he said loudly and confidently. 'Now what do you want from me?'

The angry tone had gone from the captain's voice when he spoke. He stood stiffly to attention. 'As the Comrade General knows, reactionary elements have been causing

223

unrest all over the Zone today. In the town of —— which is the Comrade General's divisional area, some of these fascist elements have seized and successfully held the factory. The People's Police sent to disperse these elements have failed to control the situation. Therefore I should like to request the Comrade Captain to send some of the Comrade General's divisional units to undertake the task.'

Finished, the M.V.D. Captain stared ahead woodenly, his eye fixed on a spot on the wall slightly above the general's head. Inwardly the room was gasping. This would definitely become another part of the Telegin legend: an M.V.D. officer addressing him in the archaic form used in Tsarist days and standing to attention to do it – like some – some Kulak!

The general acted as if nothing had happened. He clicked his fingers at the young lieutenant by his side: 'Telephone.'

The lieutenant brought a bright white telephone which seemed out of place in that company, and held it in readiness before the general.

'Get me the Third Battalion!'

The young lieutenant got the Third Battalion and held the mouthpiece while the general spoke. 'Telegin here. Yes. Three troops of your battalion ready to move off within the hour, Major. Three other troops to stand by at fifteen minutes notice. Clear?

'Good. I'm sending you over three M.V.D. officers. They will help you. I expect you to have the place cleared within one hour of arrival. Is that clear, Major? Good.'

He replaced the telephone and dismissed the lieutenant with another click of his fingers. He turned back to the M.V.D. officers again.

'My orderly officer will take you over to the Third Battalion. Is that clear?'

They clicked their heels together.

'And don't forget, Comrades, I expect to hear glowing accounts of your prowess in the attack.'

The three M.V.D. officers turned and left the room without a word.

The general waited for the door to shut, looked round the room and threw back his head and laughed, revealing a mouthful of steel teeth.

'Well, brothers, didn't I tell you I was a man! Come on, what are we waiting for. ORDERLY! More drink!'

It was dark in her bedroom, but the shaft of light that came from his own room showed her lying on the big bed. He stood there naked and watched her, feeling his own body heavy and full.

She was still dressed and in her sleep she had forced up her skirts at the side, revealing a long line of thigh, delicately chiselled and rounded where the bone met the flesh. The turgid surge that no amount of drink could subdue mounted and thickened inside him.

He had had the woman for a whole month now, ever since his division had taken over this area. She had been the mistress of his predecessor, and probably the mistress of his predecessor too. He couldn't imagine how many hands she had been through since the war had ended. This had been her house once. Now she came along with the house, like another piece of furniture.

His predecessor had been the commander of a Siberian Rifle Division; a squat, wizened man, whose tastes had been liberal, fluctuating with the availability or otherwise of women. He had brought Telegin into her room and they had watched her through the crack in the door while she dressed. He had seen the look on Telegin's face, and had laughed to himself so that his eyes seemed to disappear in wrinkles.

'She's yours,' he'd chuckled. 'All yours now, Comrade General. Yours for the taking.' He had rolled his eyes and thrust his hands up, palms outwards. 'There has never been anything like it. Like soaking in warm milk!' He made a gesture with his thumb and forefinger. 'Think of her now. Warm and soft like a baby from the bath. Look at those breasts. Think of it – slipping your hands round them from the back, warm and yielding to your hands.'

But Telegin didn't. Not that night. Nor the night after it. Nor the night after that. For the whole month he had lain in his room at nights and thought of her, torturing his nights hotly with his knowledge of her body. And now he watched her in her bed and thought of these things.

She was beautiful. Beautiful as he'd never seen a woman in Russia beautiful. She had a quality about her which the Germans called 'rassig' – a kind of supreme purity of breed.

Suddenly he realized she was no longer asleep. She was watching him; he could feel it. He felt her watching him, her breathing even and controlled. Naked as he was, he walked over to the light-switch and turned it on.

'Good evening, Telegin,' she said in bad Russian. 'Didst thou have a pleasant party?' She was cool and uninterested in his nakedeness.

'Look,' he said, and grasped the paper-backed book that lay on the table. The muscles of his arms swelled and he tore it in two. 'I can do this and much more. I can bend a silver coin in my teeth. I can look through people as if they were made of glass. I am afraid of no one. People are maggots in warm manure. But I am Telegin. And I am afraid of no one. Why wilt thou not be my woman?'

The woman moved her legs slightly and her skirt slipped from her knees.

'But I am thine, Comrade General,' she said softly. 'If thou want'st me.'

'Not like that,' the general growled. 'Thou know'st how I want thee to come to me. But not like that – like a woman of the street.'

'But don't I earn my keep on my back, like any one of them?' she said. Her voice sank to a whisper which was the parody of the approach of a whore. 'Don't talk, General.

Take. Take me like thy predecessor, General Rolishov. He took me in the stable among the horses, and the manure was still warm. Or his predecessor, below in the billiard-room on one of the tables, with three of his officers looking on.' She waved a hand to him and beckoned him to come forward. 'Come. Take me.'

'No! Not so!' he said harshly. 'Look!' The general pointed out of the window at the huts built in the courtyard. 'Down there live our women – clerks, nurses, secretaries and the like. Tonight I could ring my bell for one of them – for any one of them – and they would come gladly, even the most pure. And they would come for love, and not for fear. Because it would be with Telegin. With Telegin they would do this, although it is not common in my country.' He struck himself hard on his strong white chest, bare of any hair.

'But why dost thou want more, General?' she asked softly. 'Take me as I am. Come now – now!' She settled herself back in the deep bed, her arms under her head, her eyes haunting him to come. 'Come,' she whispered urgently. 'Come, I need thee – badly!'

He could not force his eyes away from her body, and the muscles of his stomach and arms went rigid and hard like iron, as he fought to control himself.

'No,' he said, his voice lacking strength. 'No, not like this. Thou must ask me, but not like that. Not like that. Dost thou hear?'

'How then, Comrade General? Like this, perhaps?' She jumped to her knees, the bed squeaking beneath her and clasped her hands together as if pleading for a favour. 'Dear Telegin. Please come to me, little sparrow. Come to me, my cheetah. Come now,' she thrilled the words.

He almost ran across to her, and then he was slapping her across the face, his hatred feeling satisfied in this outlet for his desire. She fell back on the bed, her head deep in the soft pillow.

'Thou wilt come,' he said, through gritted teeth, his arm-muscles still clenched with the effort. 'Thou wilt come.'

He could feel himself sweating all over.

The pain of the blows caused the tears to spring to her eyes, but her face did not lose her smile.

'Is the Comrade General losing his temper?' she said, as softly as before.

Telegin looked at her, murder in his eyes. At that moment he knew full well that he would have killed her if he had had a weapon in his hands. He controlled himself with difficulty. He felt the desire to rip every last stitch from her body and then beat the soft white flesh until she screamed with the pleasure and pain of it.

'Thou–' he began savagely, then stopped himself. He stood looking at her a moment. Without a word, he turned and went into his room, slamming the door after him.

The woman felt her burning face in the dark and then she began to cry like a child.

CHAPTER SIXTEEN

It was during the night that they first heard the clatter of tracks and the roar of engines. Everywhere the men bedding down behind the wall and between the machinery woke up startled. And everywhere the word formed on their lips.

'Panzer! Tanks!'

Richard was at the wall with Von Kornfeld. It was their spell of duty. With a great roar as the driver accelerated, the first tank came stiffly round the corner. They looked at each other for a moment and then began to count them as they moved forward into line at the bottom of the hill. Then the tanks throttled down and stopped where the trucks of the remaining people's Police made a barrier of light round the base of the hill.

'Six,' Richard said.

'Yes, and here come the infantry.'

Round the corner came four truckloads of helmeted infantry, their helmets sparkling dully in the yellow light of the deserted street.

'Four of them,' Von Kornfeld said.

'With those cannon they could make us into apple-sauce,' Richard said.

Von Kornfeld shrugged his shoulders. 'It doesn't matter, anyway.' He was tired and not concerned to hide his feelings.

Richard looked at him from the corner of his eyes.

'But I don't think they will risk damaging their precious factory,' Von Kornfeld said. 'They wouldn't use cannon for that reason.'

'Yes, I think you're right, but they could easily use them as shields for their infantry to get close enough to battle their way in.'

'It is possible. Everything is possible.'

They both watched the tanks for a few moments.

'Von Kornfeld, would you help me with the projector if I asked you?' Richard inquired.

'Yes, if my help is of use to you.'

'It is, and I am asking you now,' Richard said with a smile.

'Good.'

Everywhere the men were crowding the wall to see the tanks. Richard looked at their faces in the half-light, and hated himself bitterly again for the mess he had got them into. He looked at their faces, and saw in them fear and yet optimism. They still thought they would come through this successfully. He couldn't stand it, and went to fetch the projector.

He pulled off its sacking cover and the men watched him, as if it were purposeful action, contributing another bit to the victory that would soon be theirs. He wanted to drop the thing and tell them – shout it out loud. 'We're finished! Can't you see! We've had it! We're kaput, finito, fertig, fini, finished!' But he didn't. He went on uncovering the six-foot-long projector. He slung it over his shoulder and seized one strap of the box of rockets. He nodded to Von Kornfeld to take up the other strap.

The old man came across, rifle in hand. 'Wohin?' he asked, looking at the projector.

'Through the gate and out to the tower,' Richard said. 'Here is not good for our shot. It is better to hit them from the side.'

'You mean the tanks.'

'Yes, the tanks.'

'Richard,' he heard the girl shout.

'Yes,' he said, turning round and trying to ignore the men near him.

She pushed her way through and laid her arm on his sleeve. She said nothing, but looked up at him the whole time.

'It will go good,' he said gently and released himself from her grasp. 'It will go good.'

She turned her head away and did not see the gate-house lights go out so that the two men could leave in safety.

They crouched down behind the truck blocking the gateway and then ran heavily with their load across the thirty or so metres that separated them from the tower, the box jolting up and down jerkily on its straps. They were not fired upon.

'Here,' Von Kornfeld said and they crouched and moved into the tower through a hole in the side. It was dark inside, and placing the box on the floor, Richard lit his cigarette lighter and looked round.

The tower was in good repair considering that it was nearly four hundred years old and had been derelict for over eight years. Von Kornfeld pointed to the narrow flight of stone stairs at the wall that led up into the darkness. 'Up there,' he said. 'There is a good narrow window and the floor is strong.'

Richard shook his head. 'No, I do not think so. The angle is too great from up there. Down here is, I think, the best.'

'Yes, that is true. I didn't think of the angle,' Von Kornfeld said.

'It is some time ago that you had to do

that kind of thinking,' Richard said.

They crossed the rotten wooden floor, already holed in several places, with the long weeds growing through. Richard looked out of the narrow stone-rimmed window.

'It will give a good view of the road,' Von Kornfeld said.

'Fine. And here we will have them from the side too. The side is softer than the front. I remember the difficulty it was with the glacis-plate of your Panther. The shot just bounced off.'

'It was a good tank,' Von Kornfeld said.

'But its gun was too small.'

'It had the speed, though.'

'But in bad conditions–'

Suddenly they both laughed. 'It is funny,' Richard said. 'Here the two of us are making ready to fight the last war again.'

Richard negotiated the long tube through the narrow window, took it up in the firing position and rested it on his shoulder.

'You will put the rocket in there,' he said, turning his head to Von Kornfeld, feeling the cold metal against his cheek.

Von Kornfeld nodded his head.

'But I warn you not to stand directly behind the projector. The blast and the flame would not do you any good.'

'I had anticipated this.'

After a time Richard rested the projector on the window-sill and they sat down on the floor. He lit his last cigarette and smoked it, cupped in his hand. When he judged that he had smoked half, he passed it over to Von Kornfeld. He continued smoking the cigarette in the same manner.

'When do you think they will come?' he asked after a while.

Von Kornfeld smoked on for a while before he answered, not willing to lose any of the pleasure. 'Dawn as usual. Dawn must always bring death as well as life.'

'How will they come? Do you know that?'

'First will come the tanks, of course, and then the infantry. They will be packed and silent. And they will come slowly, like peasants ploughing a field. After a while they will shout "Hurrah", and then they will begin to run, as if they are glad now that it has come to them and as if they want it to come quickly and be finished with.'

'I have read of them like this,' Richard said.

'It was always so in my time,' Von Kornfeld went on. 'For four years I saw them come like that every morning. In the snows before Leningrad and in the heat of the

Caucasus, and always they were there in their grey coats and their long bayonets waiting to die.'

He paused and took a long last draw at his cigarette. He stubbed it out and was about to put it in his pocket. Then he threw it on to the floor. It wasn't necessary to save any more now.

The time went slowly. It was cold and Richard's feet were like ice. He wished he dare take off his shoes, but he dare not, though he knew his feet would be useless the next day. The next day; he repeated the words softly to himself and laughed. If there were going to be a next day! He yawned and stretched out his cramped body.

'Are you awake?' Von Kornfeld called softly.

'Yes. Have you not been asleep?' Richard asked.

'No, I have been lying here thinking.' Von Kornfeld paused as if he expected Richard to say something, but he did not. 'I used to live here, you know.'

'Yes, old Krause told me.'

'So. This used to be the children's part of the house when we were children.'

'We?'

'My brothers and sisters. They are all gone

238

now, of course,' he added hastily. 'Der Krieg.'

'Are you the only one left, then?' Richard asked.

'Yes, four hundred years or more of us, and now we are going to stop. Never important, but we were always there in the history of Germany.'

'And I,' Richard laughed. 'I don't even know who my grandfather was.'

'Perhaps it isn't important for you. Perhaps it isn't important at all. But in my family it always was. When we were children we were given our family tree and had to learn it by heart. And on Sunday afternoons my father would send for us one by one to his study and ask us questions on it. It was like going to church for us.'

'Yes, I suppose I can understand the importance of it for you,' Richard said slowly. 'It is important to belong somewhere, feel part of something, believe. I am afraid that I have never done.'

'Yes,' Von Kornfeld said expectantly, but Richard let the conversation die away, and Von Kornfeld leaned back against the wall and closed his eyes, though he did not sleep again.

It was easier in many ways when you

belonged, Richard thought. You had an attitude then. You had an answer pat. You had an action ready. They could never catch you out. But his father had belonged all right and they had caught him out all right. There had been nothing great in the way that he had belonged. To the dogs on a Friday night. To the pub with its beer and darts. To the gang with its hard work and accidents. He had belonged to the millions of washed, shaven-faced workmen in clean patched overalls. And then later he had belonged – all too well – to the queues outside the 'Change' in their cloth caps and crossed mufflers, and to the men on the doorsteps spitting into the gutter through their teeth.

Richard remembered the times his father had walked twenty and thirty miles in a day looking for a job. How he'd spent whole nights awake in winter waiting for the snow so that he'd be first out in the morning looking for the snow-shovelling jobs. 'Nice morning, missus. Ah, well, the kids like it, don't they? Do yer front for yer, missus! Packet of Woods and a cup o' tea!' He remembered how his father had always turned back his first day's pay to the foreman for a chance of a few days' casual labour. Working a whole day for nothing carrying bricks up and down on his head and at night his hair coming out in handfuls when he pulled off his cap and his silk-stocking pad. He'd belonged all right, but it hadn't done him much good.

In the stone-walled room it was getting light. Richard was able to make out the walls for the first time. It was nearing dawn. Von Kornfeld got up again, with a stifled groan, and urinated against the wall for the second time in half an hour. Richard felt the need too, but he told himself it was only nerves and did not get up.

Suddenly a great feeling of panic over-whelmed Richard, and desperately he wished to feel that this was all for some purpose; that everything had a purpose. He wanted to believe that this was more important than just a day's headline in a morning paper that you read after you had first finished with the sports page. The desire strained at his muscles and made the sweat stand out on his forehead in little droplets. And then it went and he relaxed and laughed at his own foolishness.

'Man,' he said out loud in English. 'If there were a God, this would be a fine time to start praying!'

'Bitte? Please?'

241

'Nothing. I'm just reviewing my past life, as they say. It's like a film you might see in the Steen in Antwerp,' he said, still in English.

'Wie bitte? Ich habe Sie leider nicht verstanden. Ich kann kein Wort englisch.'

'Well, you know how it is. They say it all flashes in front of you, and so I'm letting it flash. "All our yesterdays" and all that.' He stopped suddenly and ran to the window. Down below someone was trying to start a tank engine. There was a dry grunt. Another and then a dull roar, which was throttled down the next moment, then the engine came to life. One after another the others came to life.

'Sorry,' he said in German.

'I understand,' Von Kornfeld said seriously.

Richard blinked his eyes rapidly to clear them, and then peered out of the window again at the dark, limp silhouettes against a sky painted a dirty white by the dawn.

'I should like to drink something,' he said, and rubbed his lips.

'It is of little value in the morning. It turns to bile in your stomach. Also I do not believe in it before a battle.'

'Maybe you're right, but I could certainly

use one now.'

He placed the projector on his shoulder and peered through the square sight. They were coming. First the tanks in a rough line, two close together on the road, two on either side of the road. Behind them, so close that the mud and stones slung up by the tank tracks landed in their midst, came the infantry: slow and plodding, seemingly without spirit.

For one brief moment Richard could not believe it was happening. It was like a scene from a film. He even imagined that he could hear the infantry coughing drily, like men do in the early morning. Then suddenly he was wide-awake and clear-eyed, his sight through the projector at once intense and acute.

'I shall fire when they are about twenty metres away, to make sure,' he said, without taking his eyes off the tanks. 'It is close, but I must get them from the side if it is at all possible.'

'I agree,' Von Kornfeld said quickly.

'Then I shall hit the nearside one of the two on the road. I hope it will swerve and hinder the progress of the other. The road is very narrow. Here I shall require quick loading from you. The next two shots will be for the two tanks on the far side of the road. We cannot afford to have them get down in a hull-down position. It would be fatal.'

'And the two on this side?'

'We shall do them last – if we should live that long. I'm taking a chance that everything will be confused and that the nearside two will have little space to manœuvre. Perhaps they will crash into one another if we have any luck at all.'

'And if my grandmother had wheels she would be an omnibus.'

Richard tried to laugh, but it wouldn't come. Still, he was grateful to Von Kornfeld.

The tanks crawled slowly up the hill. They were halfway up when the firing started from the factory. Here and there a greycoated figure fell into the muddy, torn-up tracks, but the progress of the line did not falter, even a little. Von Kornfeld inserted a rocket into the end of the projector and stared out over the American's shoulder. This would be as good a place as any, he thought. Even better than most, he told himself ruefully. The tower and I. Both of us together, and that'll be it. *Basta!*

The tanks were only fifty metres away now. He could see the American's shoulder rise slightly as the muscles tightened and prepared to take the shock of discharge. Von Kornfeld picked up another rocket and cradled it in his arms, ready to slide into the tube.

They were thirty metres away. He could see a white blur peering out of the slit of the nearest tank.

And then, at last, the flat crack-boom of the projector, followed by a vicious tongue of flame back into the darkened room. A light yellow, red-fringed ball of flame exploded on the side of one of the tanks crawling up the road. It stopped dead the moment it was hit and wedged its neighbour in with it. Both crews started to jump out, as black oily-tinged smoke poured out of the vehicle.

'IN,' Von Kornfeld shouted and rammed home the next rocket.

With a heave of his shoulder-muscles Richard switched the projector to the next target and fired again.

'IN.'

The projector fired again.

Over the American's shoulder Von Kornfeld could see the black-tinged, blood-red flames licking dryly at the morning air as one of the far-side tanks started to burn fiercely.

The next instant the first shell burst, some ten metres from the tower. The walls shook as if they were alive and a hail of earth and metal pattered against them.

'IN,' Von Kornfeld screamed above the noise. 'IN! IN! IN!' And Richard fired again and again and again.

Outside everything was smoke and confusion. The burning tank exploded and tracer ammunition shot dizzy white zig-zags out of the smoke into the morning air. One more tank came to a halt. Another shell shook the tower to its foundations, sending stones from the ceiling crashing down around them.

A tank appeared out of the bright white smoke.

'It's close enough to bayonet us!' Von Kornfeld shouted above the noise.

The great weighted gun felt its way through the smoke and then swung in their direction like it does in a film when the muzzle gradually takes up the whole screen, making it into one metallic, grooved hole. Fascinated, Von Kornfeld looked along the bolts on the muzzle-brake. It fired and the air was split apart and the earth started coming up in a red-black roar from beneath them. Around them the old walls moved and came apart as if they had been made an hour before without mortar…

Von Kornfeld was bleeding from nose, ears and eyes. He had been flung against the wall by the blast, and his whole face felt like a raw beaten steak. He rasped and coughed up the taste of explosive that filled his mouth. He was alive.

He sat up and collected his thoughts. Outside all was still, except for the far-away crackle of flames burning up the air. The American? He looked around. Richard lay still under a pile of bricks and mortar. He crawled over to him and started to pull the bricks from the still body.

The American was alive. He could see he was alive. He half-uncovered the body. The arm, which was bloody and tattered, still held the crumpled projector. Richard groaned and opened his eyes. They were alive and awake at once. For a moment they sparkled in recognition, and then they grew blurred and liquid with pain.

'My arm. Is it buggered up?'

'The second one must have broken it,' Von Kornfeld said hoarsely, his mouth dry and bitter-tasting still. Steadily he worked on, freeing the American from the bricks that held him. As he worked, he told himself it again and again. He was alive. The tower had gone, but he was alive. At that impossible range and still he was alive. He was alive!

'It's very quiet,' Richard said thickly.

'Yes. They have gone now. I think.'

At last Richard was free. 'Help me up, please,' he said.

Von Kornfeld helped him to his knees and they crouched there in the grey stone rubble and stared into the white cloud that obscured the hill.

'A smoke screen?' he asked.

'Yes,' Von Kornfeld said. 'From cannon-fire it would not last so long.'

Richard felt his arm. Just underneath the elbow the sharp end of his bone was sticking up under the skin. Sweating heavily, he ripped up his sleeve while Von Kornfeld looked on. A great multi-coloured bruise caked with blood spread half-way down his forearm. In its middle the skin was drawn taut and white to a peak.

'It is broken,' Von Kornfeld said.

'Yes.' He thought a moment. 'Will you do it for me?'

'You mean the break?'

'Yes. I cannot go around with it like that.'

He picked up a piece of stone, rubbed it on his trousers and put it in his mouth.

'I take the wrist and pull hard, yes?' Von Kornfeld said.

Richard nodded.

Von Kornfeld got to his feet and then wedged his foot against the great stone that separated him from Richard. Bending down, he seized Richard's wrists in his hands.

'Now,' he said sharply and pulled hard. Richard gave a scream and spat out the stone.

Von Kornfeld let go, and Richard sank back limply on to the heap of rubble. Sweat stood out thickly along his forehead. The bruise started to bleed thinly. He lay there a long time, and Von Kornfeld watched him anxiously.

At last he got to his knees again, and together they watched the white smoke thin and reveal three deserted machines with their covers flung back at turret and bonnet, their broken tracks and the great torn and twisted splay of gleaming new metal where the rockets had holed them.

The far one was still smoking heavily, the smoke being turned stiffly at an angle of forty-five degrees by the morning breeze. Here and there was the body of a soldier;

the flaps of his long grey coat moved slightly by the wind. Otherwise there was no movement except for a tank which was backing slowly downhill, zig-zagging noisily from side to side.

'Wit haben's geschafft!' Richard said.

'We've done it,' Von Kornfeld echoed the words happily, and for the first time in many years he gave a real smile; a smile one gives rarely in adult life, broad and unqualified, so that the whole face lit up.

'You must help me,' Richard said and began to struggle to his feet. 'We must get back to the factory again before the firing starts.'

Von Kornfeld helped him to his feet and then looked around quickly. He rested his hand on a stone for a moment. It felt cold, rough and unreceptive. It was just stone and nothing else.

'Yes,' he said. 'Let's go quickly. It is dangerous here.'

CHAPTER SEVENTEEN

Telegin half-sat on the edge of the table, his legs dangling down, and poked his ear with a match-stick. While he waited for the telephone to ring, he watched her, as she stood at the tall window and looked out at the garden.

The light, silky material of her dress outlined the contours of her buttocks clearly. They were round and firm. He felt the desire to get close to her. Perhaps to slide his hands beneath her arms from the back and clasp her fine, well-formed breasts. The thought warmed him all over, starting from somewhere near his navel, but he controlled himself and forced the match-stick in his ear once more. After a moment he scraped the wax off the match-stick with the edge of his fingernail and got to his feet. Idly he strolled round the room, looking at the bookshelves that lined the walls.

He stopped and picked up a book. He opened it and turned the pages. They felt light and fragile in his big hand. He appeared very awkward to himself.

'What hast thou there?' the woman said.

Telegin did not look up. 'A book,' he said surlily.

'Good. A book. And what is the name of the book?'

He concentrated, his brow wrinkled in a frown. It was difficult. 'Narziss … and…,' he said slowly, slurring and softening the German.

'And Goldmund,' she said, completing the title for him.

'Thou knowest that I do not possess the German,' he said a little angrily.

'Don't be angry,' she said. 'It is a good book.'

'What kind of book is it – a text-book?'

'No, it is fiction,' she said.

'Fiction – what is this?'

'A thing of the imagination. Something that has not really happened. Something the writer has made up.'

'Huh,' he grunted. 'A book!' He threw it on the sofa. 'Books are for women and school-boys. Books are not for men!'

'What art thou interested in then, Comrade General?' she asked gently.

'What am I interested in?' he said gruffly. 'What should I be interested in? War, women and drink, in that order. For a man these things are of first importance. Men who believe different are not true men!'

'Comrade General, if all the men of thy nation were so, they would be the masters of the world,' she said.

'They are all so,' he said proudly.

She shook her head. 'No, that is not true. They try to believe so, but they only mislead themselves. Many are only hollow men. Many have spirits so taut that they snap like dry wood in high summer when you step on it.'

He grunted. 'My spirit thou would'st not snap so quickly,' he said.

Then the telephone rang and Telegin picked it up. He clicked over the switch so that he could speak and listened intently to what was being said at the other end. He nodded his shaven head several times and then asked sharply. 'What? Repeat that?'

His face was suddenly very serious. 'What – three? It is impossible!' He flushed red. 'I shall tell you what to do next, Comrade Captain! Fire the workers' quarters! Yes, that's what I said – fire the workers' quarters! That'll bring the animals from their rat-holes!'

Telegin breathed out deeply. 'Yes, I shall

come myself. Expect me in an hour's time.' He was about to put the phone down, but remembered something. 'And arrest Troop Lieutenant Moshno at once! He's dead! Well, then, it is not necessary!'

He clapped the receiver down angrily in its cradle. The woman could see him fighting to control his rage, his thick fingers clenching and unclenching convulsively.

'Thou!' he said suddenly and turning to face her. 'Get ready. We go in five minutes!'

'But where?'

'To see death,' the General said grimly. 'To see death as it is in life and not the way it is in books!'

2

As the first house began to burn, a man shouted from the wall, 'There's a fire!'

'A fire!' they shouted. 'Where?'

It was like a memory from another existence. A fire – a few hours' sensation in the back streets, with the children and the men, who were on the night shift, leaning out of the bedroom windows. And the owners of the house that was burning fussing over the poor battered pieces of furniture brought out into the light of day after so many years of being hidden, conscious of the eyes of the neighbours. A fire in a back-street, providing a few hours excited chatter and a few hours more of gossip.

'It looks like the Grosse Allee!' the man who had first reported the fire shouted.

'That's where you live, Jupp,' somebody said.

A big man, with a puffy, dirty white burn across the length of his right cheek, pushed forward. He peered out down at the town and a puzzled look spread over his face slowly. 'Yes, that's the Allee all right!' he said.

'Hey, lads, there's another one over here!' the man at the wall shouted again.

'Where?'

'It looks like the Scharnhorststrasse.'

And then more and more shouts from the wall. 'Here and here!' 'And over there!'

Richard, sitting on a backless chair in the middle of the yard, enjoying the afternoon sun and nursing his arm, which was beginning to hurt, got to his feet awkwardly and went over to the wall. The girl followed him.

'What is it, Richard?' she said. 'What is the matter with them all?'

'I don't know exactly,' he said slowly, but in his brain the terrible answer was already beginning to form. 'But I think that they–'

'They're burning our houses!' somebody shouted suddenly.

'What?'

'They're burning the lot down!'

A low unnatural groan went up from the men and grew into a roar of rage and helplessness. A dozen fires had broken out in a semi-circle of flames round the edge of the workers' district.

'My God,' Richard said weakly in English and leaned against the wall.

There was a loud metallic crackle and then a huge voice broke into and drowned their cries:

'Hoert ihr Verraeter! Hoert ihr Verraeter! Listen, traitors! We are burning your houses! We are burning your houses! It is just punishment! It is what you have earned by your crimes against the socialist state! But we will be humane! Come out now and we will let you put the fires in your homes out! Come down now and we will let you put the fires–'

Suddenly the man who had first reported the news levelled the captured machine-gun and fired a long burst in the direction of the loudspeaker van. The speaker stopped abruptly, but the man still continued firing until someone levered his hands away from the trigger.

'Die Hoellenhunde! Die Hoellenhunde!' the man shouted over and over again.

Richard looked at Stine, but she was staring with her father at the patch of green just outside the town where their house stood.

He waved for Von Kornfeld to come over. Von Kornfeld forced his way through the men, who stared silently across the town, not caring that they were exposed to the fire of the soldiers below.

'It is of no use,' he said. 'They would surely start firing at us once we opened the gate. Do you think so too?'

'Yes, I agree,' Von Kornfeld said wearily. 'I agree.'

'Will you tell them that, then?' Richard said. 'The old man–' he shrugged his shoulders. 'They are all finished. Please tell them. They will listen to you.'

Von Kornfeld nodded and told them. They listened to him mutely, with here and there a bowed head, as he told them in the little words that can sound dead and meaningless if one wishes. And suddenly Richard knew that he was going to die and that he was glad that he was not going to die alone and that it would be among these men.

He took the girl's hand and pressed it so hard that she went white.

'Man, man, man,' the old man said over and over again, beating his clenched fist in the palm of his other hand, the tears coursing down the furrows in the wrinkled, grey-stubbled face. From the patch of green just outside the town a column of smoke rose into the air.

3

The firing of the houses continued for most of the afternoon. One by one the little houses in the workers' district went up in flames, so that by evening the small town was surrounded by a semi-circle of burning houses and the light was gradually cut off by the smoke that came from them.

From the big black Zis limousine on the side of the hill in the shelter of the trees, the general and the woman watched the factory, but the hours went by and the men expected to come running down with their hands clasped behind their heads did not appear.

In the mirror he could see her, sitting stiff and upright, her eyes hard and shining, her skin looking hot and dry, as if it would burn to the touch. She stared straight ahead up at the factory.

'That is thy death,' he said hard and biting when he realized at last that they would not come. 'Behind me in their brick boxes fighting for air in the flames, eating everything away all around them. And that is death over there.' He pointed at the crumpled, grey-coated corpses on the hill. 'With a hole in you that you can put your whole hand in up to the wrist. That is death!'

'Shut up!' she shouted suddenly, her white flushing red. 'Shut up! I don't want to hear anything more from you!'

'But you shall!' he bellowed, all his rage centering on her, and seized her jaw in his thick fingers so that she could not move, her lips pressed outwards stupidly.

But at that moment the captain in charge of the fresh detachment from the First Battalion came across. When he was near the car he coughed politely, and Telegin released the woman reluctantly. He was sweating.

The officer clicked his heels and saluted. 'It doesn't seem, Comrade General, that the reactionaries are going to come,' he reported. And then, when the general did not say anything, 'What are you orders, Comrade General?'

Telegin watched the two white spots on the woman's cheeks where his fingers had been flush with blood and resume their normal colour.

'What do you suggest, Comrade Captain?' he said absently, still fascinated by the woman's face.

The captain's face expressed surprise, for all the years of control that he had learnt in the army. The general was not in the habit of asking his officers for advice.

'We could use our tanks, Comrade General,' he said hesitantly, 'But we are liable to have the same trouble as before if we cannot use our guns.'

The general nodded numbly. And then suddenly the woman spoke in German. 'General, don't make them die. Give them another chance to come out.'

'Give them a chance?'

'Give them till tomorrow to surrender,' she pleaded. 'Please Comrade General!'

The captain looked puzzled and uneasy. He had never seen the General like this before.

'A whole night to think about – after this.' She waved her hand around the burning landscape. 'And they will come. I am sure.'

He opened his mouth to speak, but she was quicker.

'Please. Do this, General!'

The general shook his head several times as if he were waking from a sleep. 'Captain!' he barked at the officer in Russian.

The Captain nearly smiled; he was the general again.

'Yes, Comrade General.'

'Tell that political man with his machine to tell those bastards on the hill that they've got till morning to come down. If they're not down by dawn we're coming up to get them! Clear?'

'Yes, Comrade General!' the officer snapped and saluted again, his eyes on the woman. She must be damn' good in bed, he was thinking.

He turned smartly and went down the slope back to the group of tanks and trucks. In the car the two of them were silent as they waited for the message to come through.

The air crackled and the tinny voice spoke the words of the message. When it was finished, the general looked up at the factory. But behind the scarred, chipped wall of the factory all was silence. With a grunt the general bent down and started the engine. Reversing quickly out of the trees, he slammed the gear into forward and charged down the slope, sending the soldiers lounging among the trees scattering to all sides.

CHAPTER EIGHTEEN

They drove at fifty miles an hour through the streets bordering the burning workers' districts. Every now and again they passed engines and the apparatus of the town fire brigade, ready to prevent the fire spreading outside the district, but making no attempt to extinguish the blazes.

Once they had to stop for a few moments for some twenty or thirty women and children, heads bent, sullenly dragging trek-carts loaded with what they had saved of their possessions. But the People's Police stationed at the crossing recognized the general's car. They ran across the street and rushed the carts to one side. The wheel of one of the carts came off, scattering its contents about the road. One of the policemen kicked the battered articles out of the path of the general's car. He stood stiffly to attention, and they drove on.

Then they were out of town and driving through the district of villas and houses in their own grounds. The car's speed slackened. Suddenly the general slammed on the brakes and the car skidded to a halt, vibrating with the strain.

'We'll stop here for the night!' he said simply and pointed at a small villa in its own grounds. He flung open the door and got out. The woman followed. They walked quickly up the narrow path between the firs to the door of the house. The house was quite silent, and the iron shutters had been bolted down in front of the windows. The general grasped the door-handle and turned it. It turned, but the door didn't open.

The general knocked loudly. And again. But no one came. With an exasperated curse he kicked the door so that the whole house echoed with the blow.

'Wer ist da?' a frightened voice asked from beneath their feet.

They looked down.

From the barred window of a cellar a lighted candle illuminated the white face of a man peering up at them.

'Get yourself up here!' the general said.

'But who are you?' the voice protested.

'Get up here!' the general roared in German. 'You don't talk with a General of the Red Army from a cellar, man!'

There was the echo of quick footsteps

through the silent house, and a few moments later the sound of the front door being unlocked and unbolted.

Hardly waiting for the door to be opened, the general walked in, brushing aside the dishevelled man in his late thirties who stood there.

'What can I do for the Comrade General?' the man asked, attempting a smile.

The general paid no attention to him. He rested his eyes for a moment on the woman standing at the head of the cellar steps. She wore a simple button-through dress, of which the top three buttons were still un-done. He could see that she had nothing on underneath it.

'What can I do for you?' the man repeated.

'You can get out!' the general snapped suddenly.

'Get out?' the man said stupidly, and his mouth fell open. 'But, Comrade General–'

'Make legs!'

'But I am a member of the party, Com-rade General – my card's all stamped up.'

'I don't care if you're a member of the Politburo. I said get out!'

The general looked at the woman at the head of the cellar steps and knew that he could have her for the asking. The idea sent the blood coursing through his veins violently and he wanted to be rid of them so that they could be alone in the house.

'But, Sir – er, Comrade General. Like we are?' the man persisted.

'You'll go out without something else if you don't get out at once!' the general shouted.

The man turned to the woman. 'Quick, Elli, come!'

'Wait a moment!' the general said. 'Where do you keep your schnaps?'

The man hesitated.

'Quick, or I'll have your house burnt down too!'

'In the front room – in the cabinet,' the man stuttered, and grabbed the woman's hand quickly. 'Come, Elli.' And the two of them disappeared into the darkness.

The general laughed out loud, his head flung back, the poor yellow light gleaming on his steel teeth. 'Proletenpack!' he cursed in German. 'Scared of their own shadows! "I'm a Party Member, Comrade General. My card's all stamped up!" he mimicked the man's voice and roared with laughter again. 'Pack! He'd probably been hiding in the cellar all day with his woman to see which way things went!' With a measured kick of his heavy boot he crashed the front door closed and they went into the front room.

There was plenty to drink. There always was in their houses, she thought. She fetched the bottles from the massive mahogany cabinet and put them on the table. Then she went into the kitchen in search of a corkscrew. The general ripped open his tunic, loosed the top buttons of his trousers and settled back in the deep armchair.

In the kitchen she stared at the shining row of knives. Her hand strayed out, as if it were acting independent of her body and brushed them lightly. After a moment it picked one of them up. Bright and gleaming – best Solingen steel. The blade fascinated her, and then the general roared from the front room and she closed the drawer with a clatter of cutlery. His revolver would be better. She could not use the knife. She hurried back into the room with the corkscrew.

2

They had made love among the machines. She had been like a wild animal, and he had had difficulty in holding her. Her desire had been almost frightening. It was so different from the complacent routine and prepared excitement of the women that he had known in the last few years that for a time he had felt like a young man again, with no control over his body and a gasping, throttled feeling inside him. They were only a few metres away from the others, and he had to clamp his hand over her mouth at the moment of culmination to prevent her cry being heard.

And now they lay on the little burnt patch of grass in the rigid squared shadows of the machines that rose up above them, and stared lazily at the stars and told themselves they were far away from other human beings.

'Little sparrow,' the girl said, and stroked his face, brushing back the lank, damp hair where it was plastered to his forehead. He took her hand and gently kissed the inside of her palm.

'Du,' she breathed softly.

'I love thee,' he said, his voice firm and clear and decisive. 'I love thee. I know this. And I know, too, that it is not foolish after two days.'

'It is not foolish,' she said and kissed him again. 'Thou hast had many women, Richard?' she said.

'Yes,' he said. 'I am an old man.' And yet, he told himself, at this moment she seems unutterably older than I am.

'Es spielt keine Rolle – it plays no role,' she said. 'Perhaps it is good so. Thou hast had experience and can teach me much. I don't believe that I could love a man who has not had experience.'

Richard laughed a little. 'Whether it is good with experience I do not know.' He lay back again, with his sound arm beneath her head, and looked at the stars. They were soft in a light blue, warm sky. 'One does it after a time because one has to and then because it is the only way to really know a woman. Once you have had physical experience together you are allowed beneath the surface. It becomes a mental adventure and nothing more.' He laughed again. 'But perhaps thou dost not understand, Stine?'

'No, I do not think I do.'

'It is of no importance. Nothing is of much importance.'

'Nothing?'

'Except ourselves, of course. We are of great importance. That is understood of itself.'

They both laughed softly so that the others would not hear, and her laugh was a pleasant sound.

There was a sudden rattle of heavy machine-gun fire, and above their heads some wooden fitting was shattered and rained splinters and dust down upon them. He pressed her close to him, and for a few moments after the sound of the firing had died away he could feel her heart beating quickly through the material of her blouse.

'Art thou frightened, little one?' he whispered.

'Yes.'

'So am I,' he said. He thought she might laugh, but she did not.

'I am so frightened that I shall lose thee,' she said. 'This is what I am most afraid of. For us there is no life if one goes. I cannot imagine any life without thee, Richard.'

He kissed her on her forehead and held her close. This was how it was. Life simply a battle with time. Always the bloody fight with time, trying to preserve what we have. But time always defeats us – sooner or later – erasing from below from the depths of our being; erasing all memory. We are destroyed by time.

He stroked her hair for a long time, and her eyes closed, opened and closed again drowsily. Down below the machine-gun had begun again, but its rattle was muted and sleep-inducing, it seemed.

He felt her body relax, sink and go away. His good hand was dead, but he kept it underneath her head in order not to wake her again. He looked down at her face. The innocence of two days before had gone. She had called back into herself everything of her that had lain outside; had taken refuge, enclosed in her own body. She had left him.

He looked at her and restrained the desperate urge to waken her and bring her back into his own world from the alien one of sleep. He didn't want to lose her for one moment. But he might as well get used to it, he told himself. It would be a fact tomorrow or the day after that. The world didn't give you much of a chance.

He slipped his good hand from under her head and got to his feet. Behind the machines, a few metres away, they had the radio on, and he joined the group of men standing round it in silence. They were listening to the news. The radio was of the 'People's Receiver' type of the Nazi era, which would get only German stations and they had to strain to hear the words of the news from the West:

'Flags were flying in the Federal Republic today and will do so for the next three days for those in East Berlin who have given their lives for freedom.

'In East Berlin all is quiet again and the scenes of recent disorders are deserted tonight. The city is licking its wounds.

'From Magdeburg and other centres of disorder there are similar reports. All is quiet again.

'At the opening of the Federal Parliament today, the President, Dr Ellers–' the sound faded away and someone hit the wireless to make it loud again – 'said: Let us remember our German brothers who additionally to their sufferings have now by...'

Suddenly the wireless was switched off. A man had got to his feet and turned it off. It was Von Kornfeld. Richard could see his white face in the light of the oil-lamp on one of the packing-cases, as he turned. There was no protest from the men. They sat there numbly, looking down at their hands awkwardly and at one another. They were too old to get over sorrow quickly, Richard thought. If he could have seen their faces, he imagined he would still see the fires of that afternoon mirrored in them.

Behind the cover of a pile of wood they were cooking, and a voice shouted: 'The mare's soft, lads! Come and get your share if you want it!'

But the voice was lacking in enthusiasm, and though here and there a man moved, the great part of them sat there on their boxes without a comment.

Richard went to Von Kornfeld and whispered to him. Von Kornfeld got to his feet. They walked off quietly, as if they were afraid of disturbing the others. Then they were near the wall and the smell of burning grew strong again. Richard peered through a gap in the wall at the spot where the headlights of the trucks ringed the road in light. Behind them there was an impenetrable wall of darkness. The fires were no longer to be seen.

'It goes bad,' Richard said to Von Kornfeld.

Von Kornfeld shrugged his shoulders. 'It doesn't go good.'

'You heard the radio. If it is true, it means that we are finished elsewhere.'

'It is true,' Richard said.

Von Kornfeld coughed dryly and spat into his dirty white handkerchief.

'What do you think we can do?' Richard said.

'It no longer depends on us, I think,' Von Kornfeld said tonelessly.

'But isn't there any way out?' Richard said urgently and pulled Von Kornfeld to the gap in the wall again. 'Is there no way that you know of?'

Von Kornfeld let his eyes run from left to right over the area illuminated by the headlights. All pretence at wanting to fight had gone now. He gripped Richard's arm hard just above the muscle. 'Look!' he pointed. 'Over there! About a hundred metres to the right!'

Richard followed the direction of his outstretched arm.

'That depression!'

'Yes, I see it,' Richard said. 'Well?'

'Well, if anyone could get that far, there's cover right into the forest. Then there's a chance – at least a chance.'

Richard studied the ground carefully. Perhaps the depression wasn't as deep as it seemed to be. Perhaps it would provide no cover at all...

'Yes,' he said finally, 'It goes right to the trees, but – but to get that far you've got to cover a hundred metres or so, and by that time Ivan would have made firewood of you.'

Von Kornfeld did not answer.

'Sie sind nicht uberzeugt – you are not convinced?' Richard said after a moment.

'Yes, I am convinced. But when morning comes and it starts, one and perhaps two of us might get across there in the confusion before they could shoot accurately. With luck one or two, I should say.'

'One or two! But there are forty or so of us!' Richard said.

'Yes, forty.'

'But is there nothing else?' Richard demanded fiercely. 'You used to live here. You know this place like the inside of your pocket. Don't you know anything?'

Von Kornfeld shook his head. 'No, I'm afraid there are no handy tunnels. No handy ways out this time.'

They were silent for a long while after that. 'Once,' Von Kornfeld said suddenly, so that Richard started slightly. He spoke as if his thoughts were a million miles away, 'I was in a camp there just after the war, and they brought us out of the cells into the courtyard. It was snowing hard and we were blue-red with cold. And they stood us with our noses and toes to the wall until they brought the specials out. The specials for that evening were naked. I didn't know them and I did not know what they had done. All I knew was they were naked and it was snowing and they were the specials for that evening. They said nothing. They did nothing except tremble with the cold. And then the Ivan introduced them to one another as if he were the host at some party or other. He called one Mr Adam and the other Mr Eve. And we had to laugh. Some of us couldn't laugh, and the Ivan put their feet into foot-baths full of cold water later.

'The two naked men said nothing. And the Ivan said to the man he called Adam: "Hit him! Hit him in the face!"

'Adam did not do so. He must have thought it was a joke or something. At all events, he didn't do it. So the Ivan hit him between the legs with his stick. When he was picked up, the Ivan said, "Hit him" again. The man called Adam hit the man Eve. He reached out and slapped his face, but not hard – like you might slap somebody in fun. "Not like that!" the guard said, and hit Adam in the face so that his whole mouth burst into blood. Then Ivan told him to do it again.

'This time he reached out and hit Eve quite hard, and he was crying as he did it. The guard slapped him between the legs again with his stick. "Hit him harder!" he said, and then suddenly they were both at it, grunting and fighting and sweating in the snow of a Russian winter – and somewhere I could hear somebody singing and there was a smell of cooking – onions I think – from their barracks.'

His eyes came to life for a moment as he looked at Richard. 'That's how I conceived the world until today, Mr Burdon,' he said slowly. 'I don't know exactly what my family and what my class stood for, but I know it didn't stand for that. If that was the new world, I didn't want it.'

He breathed out heavily, and his voice sank. 'So I decided that I should go from it like everything else that had belonged to me had gone too. But yesterday, after the tower, I no longer wanted to die. I wanted to live. I want to live, Mr Burdon.'

His whole face suddenly lit up with the desire for life. It was not the frightened animation of a coward, but of a man who wished for the good things that life can give. 'Mr Burdon–'

'I don't know,' Richard said lamely. He felt deflated and without life. He was empty. He could no longer give. He no longer wanted any more privileged glimpses into the hearts of his fellow creatures. In the course of his

adult life he had had too many oppor-
tunities to do that. He didn't want to any
more.

'It's no good, I suppose.' Then, suddenly
determined, 'I'm going back to sleep, Von
Kornfeld. I feel like a wet sack. And you?'

Von Kornfeld laughed a little ruefully. 'I
think I'll stay here and wait for the dawn.
Stupid, isn't it? I never thought I'd worry a
lot when the time came. And now here I am
wanting to have every minute of it – every
bit that we've got left.'

'You might be the one to do the run,'
Richard said.

Von Kornfeld shook his head. 'No, not
me.'

Richard turned and went back to the
machines. He circled the men, still sitting
round the silent radio. He did not want to
see their faces. Perhaps one or two, he
thought again, and lay down beside the girl.
She turned in her sleep and nestled into his
chest. He put his good arm under his head
and held her to him with the other one.
Above him the stars burnt softly in the light
blue of the summer sky...

The general was drunk. He had finished one and half bottles alone, and now he was drinking liqueurs – the only drink that was left. She hoped it wouldn't make him sick so that he would sober again.

She glanced at her watch. It was nearly three. She would have to do it soon. In an hour it would be dawn. Soon.

She poured herself a glass of the thick red liqueur with the sharp taste of rum. 'Prost Generalchen!' she said, and raised her glass in toast.

Telegin laughed thickly and downed his glass in a gulp. She poured him out another and took hers more carefully. She needed it. Every sip helped, although she had almost reached the stage – that warm, confident, drunken state – where nothing could fail.

'Can I come to thee?' she asked, and tried to give her face the warmth of a promise.

'Come,' he said, stretching out both hands from the sofa. 'Come.'

She went over to him, and before she could sit down he had pulled her over him. His thick, stubby fingers travelled all over her upper body. She simulated passion, breathing quick and loud.

'Thou hast come!' he said thickly. 'Now.' Seizing a handful of the stuff of her blouse, he jerked at it. It didn't tear. Clenching his jaw, he pulled at it again with all his strength. The material ripped down to the waist, cracking like a rifle-shot.

Trying wildly to keep her head, she told herself she must get the revolver. Her whole body was screaming with the desire to surrender to him. She felt her legs dissolve away into nothing. Her heart was beating madly. With fumbling fingers she felt for the holster hanging down somewhere near the floor. She found it, but the catch was stiff and it wouldn't open. She moaned low in her throat. Her whole body trembled. It shouted for satisfaction. And then the cold metal burnt like ice into the palm of her hand. She left herself fall to the floor, and the next moment she was crouching there on her knees, revolver in hand.

'What art thou doing?' he shouted, startled.

She said nothing. She still could not control her breathing, and her eyes refused to focus properly.

His drunkenness seemed to fall from him like a piece of clothing. The tenseness came and went from his face. He leant back in the sofa again and laughed. 'Oh! So you are going to kill me!' His eyes did not leave her face! 'The little bourgeois heroine is going to kill the bad Soviet general, eh?' He relaxed even further into the soft pile of the sofa. 'Well, go on. Kill me,' he said calmly. 'Kill me, if you are not afraid.'

'Shut up!' she shouted. 'Shut up! I'm not afraid of you! Once I was afraid of you and your nation! But not now! You have nothing to bring but death! Nothing!' Her breasts heaved with effort.

He laughed. 'Did you think we had anything else to bring? Of course not! We bring death. But, then, death is important! Nothing else. Death is what we all desire, really! We'll show it to you…'

She fired and missed. He flung himself on her from the sofa, and she sprawled back in the deep fur of the carpet under his weight. They struggled. She freed one hand and brought her long nails down across his face and neck. His leg shot out with the pain and the small table with its light fell to the floor. The room was in darkness except for the red glow from the oven.

With one hand he grabbed her long hair, and twisted it in a knot over his fingers and wrist, pulling her face close to his. In the red glow from the trap, he saw her eyes bulge and the hair raise the skin in countless little bulges at the roots. It hurt. He knew it hurt. But her eyes refused stubbornly to show pain. She was breathing fast and shallow.

'This is what you want,' he said, breathing heavily. 'This is all you women want in the world.' He kissed her, and she bit the inside of his lips, tearing at the rubbery skin till her teeth met.

'Now you want,' he whispered hoarsely. 'Admit it. Admit it!'

'No,' she gasped. 'No!'

'Admit it.' He gasped. 'Admit it.'

She tried to hold back the words. But they came. They came, and with them her body seemed to break invisible bands that were holding it. 'Yes, yes!' she breathed, and felt the heat of his breath on her face. 'Yes,' she screamed...

CHAPTER NINETEEN

The grass was grey-green in the low ground-mist of the morning. In the trees on the far side of the road the bright dust of the sun flickered in light stains on the foliage. For that time it was warm and the bite of an early summer morning was absent. Here and there a man coughed dryly, but there was no more water; the supply had been cut off during the night. The old man in the leather coat smoked the stump of a cheap cigar and the others watched him intently.

The sun slid gradually along the concrete of the yard, and it warmed and filled the faces of the men. A bird cruised over them in the sun. The men looked up at it as it soared effortlessly in the currents of the air. It turned, and in the sun's rays the greyness of its feathers suddenly became bright and acute. A blob of white fell from it and smeared the wall.

'The bird's laid a crooked egg!' the man with the dirty white burn across his face said, and they watched it disappear in the distance.

'If I could lay a crooked egg and fly away like that!' the old man with the cigar said. But no one seemed to hear him.

For a long time the men looked up into the pale blue sky of the morning.

The old man stood by himself by the wall and stared at the little town with its new scars. He had been standing there all night. The town was silent. It could tell him nothing.

A hand tapped him softly on the sleeve. He turned round. It was the American.

'Old man,' Richard said. 'I am going to the gate.'

'So,' he said.

Richard hesitated. 'Will you come with me – it is perhaps better there?'

The old man shook his head. 'No, I stay here. I can see the town here.'

For a while Richard looked over the wall with him. Down below figures in the overalls and leather helmets of tank-men were moving around now. A tank was being fuelled up and another was having its track repaired. It was a good morning. Visibility was very clear.

Richard put out his hand – the good one.

'Goodbye, then, old man.'

The old man took it.

'Leben Sie wohl,' Richard said.

'Leben Sie wohl.'

The old man withdrew his hand quickly and turned to stare down at the town again. In the far distance a tiny train ran along the horizon, its smoke bent stiffly behind it in a long streamer. To Richard it seemed wrong that trains should be moving on this day.

Behind one of the machines Richard searched his pockets for a scrap of paper. When he had found a piece, he wrote the name of the place where she should go and then wrapped the paper in the rest of his Westmarks. For a moment he looked at the Eastmarks that he had pulled out with the other money. The coins were worthless. He threw them on the ground. He put the West-marks and the paper in his pocket.

The girl's jacket lay on the ground where they had slept, and he slipped the money and the paper with the address into her pocket and pulled the flap down securely. He would tell Von Kornfeld about it later.

Stine came back from where she had been. She looked good, although she had not been able to wash for almost two days.

'Stine,' he said, 'we must go now.'

'Where?'

'To the gate.'

'Thou has need of my help, Richard?'

'Yes, with my arm. Here.' He bent down, picked up her jacket and draped it round her shoulders. She took it off again and put it on properly.

'This is not the day for that,' she said.

They walked across the yard to where Von Kornfeld was standing, filling the magazine of his rifle from a box of ammunition.

'They are about to start below,' Richard said.

Von Kornfeld put back the magazine and tapped it to make sure it was in correctly. 'Yes, I know.'

'I want you to come with us to the gate, Von Kornfeld.'

Von Kornfeld looked at him queerly, but did not say anything. He slung his rifle, and the three of them went towards the gate.

From the wall four men came slowly, each with one shoulder hunched with the weight of their burden. They were carrying the body of the old man in the leather jacket.

'He caught it at the wall,' the man with the dirty white burn across his cheek said. 'It was that M.G.' He wiped the sweat from his

286

brow. 'He's heavy.'

'He was an old man. He didn't duck quickly enough!' someone said.

There was no mark to be seen on his face. It was whole, but surprised. Stine turned away. They went on. After a moment Richard touched her arm. She looked up at him. 'Is it always like that?' she asked.

'War, dost thou mean?'

'Yes.'

'Yes, I suppose so.'

'Then it is more terrible than I had ever thought,' she said. 'That poor old man.'

'Yes,' he said, because that was what one was supposed to say, and yet he knew, as all men know, that war is the greatest experience they ever had. He thought of the lines of poetry he had once learnt at school: 'And he is dead who will not fight, and he who dies fighting has increase.' It was probably a stupid poem in its entirety, but still the lines had stuck in his memory and seemed important.

There was the chatter of the machine-gun again, and Richard pushed Stine behind him. Von Kornfeld came up in the rear. They were quite near to the gate now.

'Keep close to the wall,' Richard said. 'We're going over to the far side of the gate.'

'Why not this side?' Von Kornfeld asked.

'I have my reasons. When I give the word, we'll run forward past the truck. Clear?'

'Klar.'

'Klar!' Von Kornfeld said.

They began to run, crouched low in line. They squeezed past the truck. The wood of the side quivered and was shattered into splinters. They ran on again, and the line of destruction followed in little jumps of dust and metal on to the road. 'In that hole!' Richard shouted and pushed Stine forward into the ditch beside the road. He flung himself in it after her. He landed on his bad arm, but felt no pain then. A moment later Von Kornfeld fell in behind him.

They lay sprawled there for what seemed a long time, panting and gasping hurriedly for breath. Then they sat up and began to observe the preparations being made for attack below at the base of the hill. The clatter of the heavy M.G. ceased. All was quiet now, except for the tinny sound of a hammer being struck against iron. Her hand stole softly into his and held it. There was an absolute silence now.

The three tank soldiers gathered round the broken track. They had wound back the length of metal to the sprocket wheel, and now they were hammering in a new tie-in. The soldier in the leather tank-helmet hammered rapidly at the metal track which moved back every time he struck it. Then it was through and they sat down, their backs against the wheels.

The tall, thin soldier with the leather tank-helmet said: 'Well, as far as I am concerned, it can start.'

The blond, stub-nosed soldier with freckles said seriously. 'Thou hast a great hurry to die, I think.'

The third soldier laughed. 'Up with your leg; Russia needs more soldiers.'

They all laughed, and then the blond soldier spat out a sunflower seed and asked seriously, 'What wouldst thou prefer most at this time – vodka, roast goose or a woman?'

'We'll get neither, so what does it matter?' the tall soldier said grumpily.

'Please,' the blond soldier said. 'I regard this as a serious question. What wouldst thou prefer?'

The tall soldier rubbed his oil-stained hand over the stubble of his chin. 'Me. I should take the vodka.'

'And thou?' He turned to the third soldier.

'Me? I should like a woman.' His eyes

flickered for a moment. 'A woman. One with white breasts like puddings.' He scratched his head reflectively.

The blond soldier laughed. 'Me. I should take all three. Vodka, roast goose and the woman. The world is ours, isn't it? I'll take the lot.'

The tall soldier in the tankman's leather helmet laughed dryly. 'I have seen them like thee before,' he said. 'All that thou will do is to let a piece of lead make love to thee.'

The whistle blew for assembly. The under-officer moved along the line of vehicles shouting orders. The tall soldier fastened the strings of his helmet and looked up at the factory on the hill.

'Poor bastards,' he said softly. Softly so that no one heard.

The general ran from the great black car. He ran with his tunic flying open, his hair disarranged, and when he came closer, the waiting soldiers could see that there were thin streaks of clotted blood running down his face, as if he had been scratched.

'Start up!' he shouted to the little group of tank-drivers.

They scrambled on to the steel bonnets of their tanks.

'Gunners, load your pieces.'

'But, Comrade General, the factory!' a squat, flabby officer objected.

Telegin gave him a push under the chin with the heel of his hand. The officer fell backwards.

'Load your pieces!' the general shouted again in the Ukrainian language.

'You, brother!' he shouted at the commander of the leading tank. 'Get yourself down and let me up!'

Quickly he pulled off his shaped tunic and threw it on to the churned-up earth. He rolled up the sleeves of his white shirt and climbed up into the turret.

'Anton Stepanovich!' he shouted.

The young lieutenant appeared.

'The bottle!'

The young lieutenant pulled a flask from his pocket and unscrewed it. He passed it up to the general. The general drank deeply and handed it down again.

'Give them all a drink, Anton Stepanovich, as far as it goes,' he shouted.

The young lieutenant ran from tank to tank giving each man a drink as far as the alcohol went. Then he flung the flask away and clambered on to the turret of the general's tank.

'Where art thou going?' the general bellowed above the roar of the starting engines.

'With you, Comrade General!'

'No! It's not for thee, little brother. Nothing for thee!' the general shouted and reached down to touch the lieutenant's hair. 'Go on! Get down!'

The tank started with a jerk that flung the general forward against the cupola rim. Stretching out both arms behind him, he brought them forward, signalling the tanks to form a line on both sides of him. Revving heavily, pouring clouds of thick blue smoke into the morning air, the tanks slowly moved forward into line.

'Weeeish–crack!' The first shell tore at the air flatly and burst the earth in front of them into a million pieces.

'They're using cannon this time!' Von Kornfeld roared into Richard's ear.

Richard nodded his understanding and looked up again at the advancing tanks. The light morning air stank suddenly and became evil.

They were a hundred metres away now. Ponderously they moved forward, lurching down now and again, their tracks throwing a stream of earth and pebbles behind them.

A crack that grew terrifyingly into a ball of red fire and exploded into a multi-coloured roaring star. A great chunk of masonry fell out of the wall behind them. It was time for them to go, if they were ever to go. The hill was becoming obscured with the smoke of the explosions, which was good.

Another shell ripped violently at the air above them, and Richard pressed the girl's head tight to his chest and wrapped his good arm round her ears. 'You!' he roared above the noise of the falling shell. 'You must take out Stine!'

Von Kornfeld's face crushed up as the shell exploded. 'How?'

'The way we talked about.'

'But it is impossible.'

The chatter of a machine-gun, and something took possession of the soil just in front of them. They thrust their heads down close to the soil.

'Now, it isn't,' Richard shouted.

'You go.'

'No! My arm – give away!'

The chatter of the machine-gun stopped for a moment and they raised their heads. Richard released his hold on Stine. The tanks were fifty metres away. The gun of the leading one moved blindly in a slow arc as if it were feeling its way.

'Quick now!' Richard shouted.

He dragged Stine to her feet. 'We're going out!'

'All of us?' she shouted.

'Yes. Going in groups! Run!'

Another explosion. Back in the factory the siren sounded. They could hear it even above the gunfire. Then they were running. As they ran, Richard flung away his machine-pistol and knocked Von Kornfeld's rifle from his hand. They ran hard, crouched low. A roar. A crash. The ground opened in front of them and they were enveloped in thick yellow-grey smoke. Stine faltered.

'I love thee, Stine,' he shouted and then gave her a push to run on.

Over their heads was the flat crack-back-crack of a big shell with a flat trajectory and behind them one of the tall metallic towers swayed and fell over. Again they were enveloped in smoke. They kept on running. Richard ran a little harder and caught up with the girl. For a moment they ran side by side and he touched her arm. 'Run! run!' he panted and then he fell behind. Von Kornfeld passed him. 'Paper in her pocket. Paper in her pocket!' he shouted above the noise, summoning his last reserves of strength.

Then they were both in front of him. He was still running. He didn't want to stop. He was still running – slower – slower. He didn't want to lose her. He wanted … he wanted … wanted. He stopped. The two of them had nearly reached the trees now. The smoke blurred the two figures and they seemed like something seen in an old film of another year. The smoke thickened and he saw them no more.

Telegrin kicked his driver's left shoulder and the tank swerved slightly, catching the holed steel wreck that blocked the road by the rear sprocket and sending it into the ditch. Telegin straightened up and peered through the smoke, his eyes wrinkled, as if in a high wind, at the factory.

Everywhere there was thick oily smoke and flames. The whole factory was quickly becoming a heap of rubble. It was the end of his career, but he didn't care. His whole body tingled with joy. The feeling was better than that of a woman. A sudden wild surge of energy, like the old days as a boy when they had emerged from the dark-green cold forest and spread out on the captured half-wild horses, running them over the bare plain for the sake of running them until they were exhausted.

He kicked his driver in the centre of his shoulders twice to indicate more speed. They lurched forward. Through the smoke he caught sight of one of his troop. The cupola was shut down tight and there was nothing to be seen of the commander.

'Coward!' he shouted out loud to the empty field, and drew himself erect in the turret so that the whole of his upper body to the waist was visible.

The smoke cleared again. A man was running heavily down the road to meet them. He was carrying a rifle. He was an old man. Telegin could see he was an old man.

The old man saw the tank. He knelt down and took aim like men who had fought in wars long ago had been taught to take aim. He seemed to take a long time. Telegin screamed something, the spittle on his lips blown away by the breeze. He turned and pulled at the machine-gun mounted on the swivel. He drew it half-round and then it jammed. He jerked madly at the gun. He could see the old man quite clearly now: brown wrinkled face, the grey stubbled cheeks, the bushy eyebrows – like the old men in his village once.

'Bitch! bitch!' he screamed at the top of

his voice at the gun. He tugged at it, exerting all his strength. It refused to come. He stared at the gun like a toy in the old man's big heavy hands. 'Bitch!' he screamed.

A terrible blow on his side and a red darkness. He fell over the gun. In his mouth was the burning salty taste of blood. He lay on the turret and saw the old man kneeling there in the path of the tank. He had lowered his rifle. Telegin wanted to shout a warning against himself. But no words came. The blood flooded his mouth and the spirit seemed to seep out of a hole in his body. In his brain a thought uncurled slowly, like a lock of hair in water...

Richard lay in a shell-hole on their flank. There were others with him in the holes that dotted the hill-top. They had run there when the factory went up in flames. But Richard told himself he was alone. Now that he knew for certain, he wanted it to be alone – not with the others. In death he wanted to feel himself something special or know that the whole world was going with him. It wasn't so, so he wanted to feel alone.

He nestled the rifle he had picked up into the hollow of his good shoulder. It became part of him. The tanks had passed and the flanks of the infantry were uncovered.

He took aim. It was too easy. Through his sight he ran his eye along the six or seven men in grey in his arc of fire. He could have anyone of them.

'The next man who comes into my sight,' he said in English. The next came and Richard fired. The man in grey flung up his arms and fell forward on his face. Richard put down his rifle and waited for them to come.

There was almost silence now, except for the shrill high sound of the siren. Here and there a wounded man groaned, and his groan was followed almost at once by a rifle-shot. The men in grey mostly used their rifles to shoot the wounded and it was awkward with the head and made much mess. They were going from body to body and turning them over.

'Dead?'

'Dead.'

Richard could hear them. He lay face down in the earth, which was warm and soft where the shell had turned it over. It was good to lie there like this, he thought lazily and felt very tired.

He thought of the girl a bit and then he

didn't think of her any more. They were getting nearer. The sun was warm on the back of his head.

'Dead?'

'Dead.'

He closed his eyes firmly and thought of the hot sun and the yellow beach and the white house by the blue sea when he'd been young. He remembered. Then he didn't think of anything any more.

'Dead?'

'Dead.'

Richard felt something hard and pointed thrust between him and the soft earth. He was turned over. He decided not to open his eyes. Far away he heard a voice ask: 'Dead?'

'Dead.'

The siren stopped.

The publishers hope that this book has given you enjoyable reading. Large Print Books are especially designed to be as easy to see and hold as possible. If you wish a complete list of our books please ask at your local library or write directly to:

Dales Large Print Books
Magna House, Long Preston,
Skipton, North Yorkshire.
BD23 4ND